THE CASE FOR A PRETRIBULATIONAL RAPTURE

Lee Y. Martin, Ph.D.

The Case For A Pretribulational Rapture

First Edition – 2022

Cover Page Design, Concept & Copy Rights

Pravallika Pasumarthi .

Bhagya Nagar 2nd Lane ,

Ongole -523 001 , Prakasam Dist,

Andhra Pradesh – INDIA

WhatsApp No : +91- 8179837381

E-Mail : podalihemu66@gmail.com.

FORWARD

All Scripture is taken from the King James Bible unless otherwise noted. Also, everything within quoted Scriptures that is bracketed, in parenthesis, italicized, emboldened, underlined, or put in caps is mine unless otherwise noted. Scriptures are heavily edited for clarification purposes for readers who are newly born again and not familiar with the Christian Bible.

ACKNOWLEDGMENTS

I believe that the Lord in His wisdom directed me to publish this treatise about a Pretribulational Rapture. He confirmed His directive to me in a prophetic message which I was not seeking a while back. God alone knows the significance and importance of this project due to all the signs and signals indicating that Jesus' return is about to happen. I am merely His hands and mouthpiece to make the doctrinal teaching of a rapture of the church of Jesus Christ, the prologue to a long-awaited Kingdom Age, understandable to the hearts of new converts to Christianity.

I want to give tremendous credit to Pravallika Pasumarthi who tirelessly and faithfully to the Lord's command edited the manuscript for this book. She convinced me that the book needed publishing due to the nearness of the event called rapture. Because I have not desired to be an author of Biblical books, she assured me that many Christians throughout the world needed to hear of this Biblical truth which she was not aware of and that she could do the work in getting it published. Indeed she has. I highly recommend her as a helper for anyone who needs assistance for help in publishing.

Table of Content

Chapter -1   1 - 24
Rapture is a Foundational Doctrine of Christianity

Chapter -2   25 - 36
How Critical is the Rapture Doctrine ?

Chapter – 3   37 - 58
Prologue to the Kingdom Age

Chapter -4   59 - 78
Comfort and Encouragement

Chapter -5   79 - 95
The Rapture in the Old Testament

Chapter -6   96 -109
Recapitulation Confirms Rapture a Worthy Goal

Chapter -7   110 - 127
Day of Destiny

Chapter – 8   128 - 139
Who is Qualified for Rapture ?

Epilogue   140 - 142

Addendum   143 - 151
How to Became a Christian

PREFACE

Because we are in the season of a rapture of the true church, this book is written to alert people unaware of the doctrinal truth about the rapture of born-again believers prior to the Tribulation which ushers in the Kingdom Age. Many Christian leaders do not subscribe to a rapture let alone a Pretribulational one and hence do not teach on it. But I believe it is a foundational Christian doctrine. You will learn why I believe it is after reading the book.

The book has come forth from a compilation of a series of papers I wrote for a website I had with a Christian colleague for twenty years. She was gifted with being able to see in the spirit world from a child. In her later years the Lord brought us together in a strange relationship.

God would visit my coworker in dreams and visions but give me interpretations for many of them. The ones for which I had the interpretation all seemed to relate to a rapture of the church. We thought this a strange happenstance until we noted that Daniel was given the interpretation of Nebuchadnezzar's dreams and Joseph was given the interpretation of Pharoah's dreams as well as the dreams of Pharoah's butler and baker while in prison.

The Lord told my colleague and I to put these visitations of His on a website in the mid-1990s. At the time, the Internet was relatively new to Christian usage so we were in the avant-garde of prophecy websites. Now the Internet is overloaded with Christian sites along with social media. As a result, much confusion abounds regarding this most important Christian doctrine of rapture exposed by Apostle Paul.

Paul was commissioned by the Lord to reveal hidden mysteries of the Old Testament, and one was the hidden truth of a rapture of the church at an appointed time. Hopefully, the chapters following will explain it simply so unschooled seekers of truth can understand it. I have tried to validate everything said with Scripture.

Because all 55 visitations on the website my colleague and I had related to the rapture, I wrote a series of papers for visitors to the site explaining it, and I posted a series of papers about Daniel's 70 Weeks Prophecy as well since they are tied together in time and context. This book will only speak to the rapture event. Due to the amount of confusion on social media concerning the subject of rapture, the Lord impressed us a couple of years ago that we should remove our website from the Internet.

I have updated and restructured papers I wrote for the website and for a ministry in India that I worked with for 30 years reorganizing them for this book published by request of the Lord. I was not seeking to publish any of them until I was encouraged to do so by a young evangelist from India who did not know about the doctrine. This astonished me.

After obtaining copies of my papers about rapture and related issues from the ministry in India, this evangelist was surprised to find the teaching as a major doctrine in the Word of God. Hence, I reconsidered publication of what the Lord has shown me over the six decades that I have been studying the Bible. Just last week I was given a prophetic oracle direct from the Lord confirming the fact that this book was His instigation and not mine as I alluded to above. This shows He is concerned people have enough knowledge with which to make a wise choice about this weird strange event called rapture so they can make preparation to participate in it.

Anyone who denies that it is a major doctrine of Christianity should tear out both of Paul's letters to the church in Thessaly. Considering that he was only in Thessalonica three weeks before being run out of town by orthodox Jews, he must have considered it a major part of his gospel of Jesus. And indeed it is since it speaks to the Lord's return. You will understand why I believe this to be true after reading the book. I can only point out and suggest what Scripture says. It is the Holy Spirit's job to reveal it as truth.

Because of the church's overemphasis about success in the temporal world as opposed to harvesting rewards for Eternal Life, and because of the awakening to spiritual matters due to covid-19, people in India and all over the world who are not familiar with the rapture doctrine ought to be afforded the information presented in this book so that they can make themselves ...*worthy to escape all the things that are coming to pass* [Luke 21:36] as revealed in the book of Revelation.

Given that the signs of the times indicate we are in the season of Jesus' return, the cost of purchasing the book is as low as possible. I am ready for departure to my heavenly home and will readily go over line by line any truth my Lord graciously shows me as I have done in this book.

Pray for wisdom and understanding as you read.

For people who want to be rapture-ready,

Lee Y. Martin, Ph.D.

CHAPTER - 1

RAPTURE IS A FOUNDATIONAL DOCTRINE OF CHRISTIANITY

This book is written to build confidence in the hope of a Pretribulational rapture. Biblical proof that believers will not go through the Tribulation period should comfort people aware of the horrors to come revealed in Apostle John's Apocalypse at the end of the Christian Bible. When I say believers, I mean truly born-again Christians who are repentant, have cleaned up their lives, quit sinning, and have separated from the world. A firm grasp of this treatise will comfort anyone eagerly awaiting our Lord's return.

Many prominent Christian leaders are promoting a false doctrine concerning the rapture. For people who do not know about a rapture let me define it. It is the translation of <u>living</u> saints to heaven in a moment of time without experiencing death. Some people say there will be no rapture, and others misplace it thinking it will happen at the end of the 7-year Tribulation or midway through it. If so, Christ's Bride will have to go through the worst time the world will ever see according to our Lord [Matthew 24:21] and the Old Testament prophet Daniel...

Daniel 12:1

12 And at that time shall Michael stand up, the great prince which standeth for the children of thy people: and there shall be a time of trouble, such as never was since there was a nation even to that same time: and at that time thy people shall be delivered, every one that shall be found written in the book.

If the Lord and righteous Daniel are correct, the naysayers about rapture imply that Christ plans to permit His Bride to be beaten up just before He marries her. I don't think so. Even though much catastrophe during the Tribulation is the work of satan, the Tribulational desolations are a work of God. He will use the devil's plots and schemes as a battleaxe to bring to pass His foreordained divine decrees against sin in like manner as Assyria was God's hammer to crush the rebellious Northern Kingdom of Israel; and Babylonia was His rod to punish the Southern Kingdom for their refusal to turn from idolatry [Jeremiah 51:20].

Is The Rapture An Escape?

Since The Lord has equipped us to live in any difficult situation, the rapture is not an escape from responsibility. But it is indeed an escape from the wrath of God because Jesus is not going to scourge His Bride before the wedding. Given that we are in the immediacy of the Tribulation, Jesus is wooing His church to clean up her act so she can become His betrothed and escape the Father's wrath. Urgency for holiness preparedness is acute because all of a sudden without any sign or warning the Lord will remove His Bride from the earth. Could this be the 'suddenly' by which earth-dwellers will be propelled into Tribulation [1 Thessalonians 5:3]?

How will it begin? The Father will tell His Son to go get His Bride – purified believers from within the body of Christ.   Jesus will come to just above the top of the mountains where He will shout for His church to come up to Him in the air. The dead in Christ will rise first, and then living believers will gather together with them in the air to meet the Lord *'in clouds'* [1 Thessalonians 4:16-17]. These are not earthly rain clouds; they are heavenly glory clouds of a different nature unaffected by temporal constraints and able to support the weight of physical objects.

The rapture event is one of the mystery doctrines Paul was given concerning the church. Being a mystery, it was hidden in the Old Testament canon out of sight. Paul wrote: *Behold I show you a mystery: we shall not all sleep, but we shall all be changed* [1 Corinthians 15:51]. Like caterpillars believers will be metamorphosed into a different creature-form matching Jesus' glorified body.

When is the change? Change is at the rapture. Who is changed? <u>Prepared</u> believers taken out of Christ's body (the church) in like manner to Eve being taken out of Adam's body at her creation. So, the Bride consists of prepared born-again believers. Sadly, there will be a lot of mourning in that day because not all believers are ready.

Mystery doctrines concerning the Church Age were given to Paul by Jesus Himself [Ephesians 3:1-3] in his oft appearances to Paul.

Acts 26:16

16 But rise, and stand upon thy feet: for I (*Jesus*) <u>have appeared</u> unto thee (*Paul*) for this purpose, to make thee a minister and a witness both of these things which

thou hast seen, and of those things in the which I <u>will appear</u> unto thee;

Paul used the rapture *episunagoge* (Greek) assemblage of Christians in the air to encourage believers not to defect from hope of missing the Tribulational wrath of God. He spoke about the rapture in both his letters to Thessaly. In his second epistle, he reminded them...

2 Thessalonians 2:1

2 Now we beseech you, brethren, by the coming of our Lord Jesus Christ and by our gathering together (*episunagoge*) unto him,...

Epi is a prefix that intensifies our *gathering together* denoting it is a very important assembly, and indeed it is for it is the day all heaven has been waiting for – the marriage of the Lamb of God. Calling up the Bride to meet the Lord in the air is the prologue to the marriage ceremony in the Father's house in heaven that will take seven earth years to accomplish.

When Jerome translated the Bible into Latin in the late 4th century, he used a derivative of the Latin word *rapere* meaning 'to seize' in order to translate the Greek word *harpazo* that means 'to seize'. Because Latin was the language of the Romans, the Latin Vulgate became the Bible of the empire. Hence, the noun rapture from Latin's *rapere* signified the catching away of people, and it became common to call the seizing of saints off earth rapture.

1 Thessalonians 4:16-17

16 For the Lord himself shall descend from heaven with a shout, with the voice of the archangel, and with the trump of God: and the dead in Christ shall rise first:

4

17 Then we which are alive and remain shall be **caught up** (*harpazo*) together with them in the clouds, to meet the Lord in the air: and so shall we ever be with the Lord.

When theologians came together for conferences and synods in the Middle Ages and later in the Reformation period, they spoke different languages but they all knew Latin, so rapture became the word of choice for the Greek *harpazo*. It naturally evolved into a theological term used to refer to the concept of seizing living saints off earth prior to the Tribulation.

In extrabiblical parlance, the Greek word *harpazo* was used of a pickpocket thief who would snatch items from people in a market place. He had to be quick, sudden, and accurate to get away with it. Probably no other word could explain more suitably the Biblical capture of saints than *harpazo* aka rapture. So, if someone says to you the word rapture is not found in the Bible, implying it is a bogus concept, tell him it is found in the Latin Bible worldwide, millions of which are still in use by the Vatican church.

Harpazo in English vernacular means to seize upon or snatch away someone with force in order to escape from something perilous just in the nick of time. No other word better defines rapturing to heaven a group of people out of earth so that they miss the coming Tribulational desecrations known in Scripture as the Day of the Lord. Chapter 3 will speak to this concept in more depth.

There are a number of instances in Scripture where *harpazo* translates the catching away and transporting of people instantly to another place. The following are a few: Enoch, Elijah, Jesus, the man-child of Revelation chapter 12, Paul in a self-described visitation to heaven, Philip caught away from the eunuch in the Judean desert and taken to the Gaza strip some 35 miles away, Isaiah taken to the throne-room to receive a message from God for the Israelites, the two witnesses revived and caught up to heaven in the Tribulation, the 144,000 sealed Israelites at mid-trib, and the group event of the Bride of Christ prior to the Tribulation.

End of the Church Age

The theological purpose of the rapture is not to begin the Tribulation, but to remove the church out of the way so God can finish the Jewish Age. There is one week left of Daniel's 70 Week Prophecy for Jews before the Kingdom Age starts. The Church Age has been a parenthetical lapse of time which God programmed for the calling out from among gentiles a people for His name [Acts 15:14]. Why did He want to do this? He wanted to reverse His disinheritance of the human race at the tower of Babel incident.

In grief, God gave men over at Babel to their rebellious desire to return to the wicked works of the world corrupted by fallen angels that caused the flood. Nevertheless, in mercy and in pursuit of His redemptive plan for mankind, God chose one man from among men, Abraham, to form a people for Himself, a nation of His own to preserve the seed of the woman from contamination due to flagrant sin as before the flood. A second equally important reason He needed a client nation set apart from others was to demonstrate to the residue of nations – by way of the Mosaic law – differences between the clean and the unclean, the holy and the profane [Deuteronomy 32:8, 9 with 4:8].

God loves all people and would like everyone to choose Him as their Lord. But they don't. Being provoked to forsake His rebellious creatures at Babel, God divided people into nations separating them via language barriers. He gave them over to unseen angelic rulers, princes from God's heavenly divine council.

Deuteronomy 32:8
8 When the most High divided to the nations their inheritance, when he separated the sons of Adam, he set the bounds of the people according to the number of the **children of Israel.**

From the above, we learn that at Babel the nations were established in righteous frustration [Genesis 10] and were divided up according to the number of the *children of Israel.* But, the authoritative Greek Septuagint Bible, written for Greek speaking Hebrews by a committee of 72 Jewish scholars, translated the Hebrew Bible into Greek around the 2nd century B.C. to read the emboldened text above as 'angels of God'. That is the better translation because it is an exact equivalence of the Hebrew into Greek. Jews ought to know the meaning of their own vernacular.

These ruling angels from God's heavenly divine council are called ... *sons of the mighty...* in Psalms 89:6 and *...watcher angels...* in Daniel 4:13 & 23. This heavenly council helps God rule His universe. When the angels and the council were formed is pure speculation. Some say it was during the theorized time gap between Genesis 1:1 and 1:2.

Regardless of the council's inception, the problem is that these mighty angelic princes given custody of the nations of earth perverted their mandate acquired at the tower of Babel and have caused the earth to become ripe for judgment again. Psalms 82 records God's indictment against them. Psalms 82 is not talking about earthly judges as some men teach.

It behooved the Lord to make a way for forsaken gentiles to escape their oppressive overlords. Thus, He engrafts worthy gentiles into His elect nation of Israel [Deuteronomy 4:20 with Romans 12:17]. Space does not permit delving any more into the study of Israelology (study of the Jewish nation) and Ecclesiology (study of the church) wherein lies the mystery doctrine of God making from two, Hebrews and Gentiles, one new man [Ephesians 2:15]. Very simply, as you will learn the church has to be raptured out of the way for God to keep His promise to Israel that she would rule the world in a Kingdom Age.

Purpose of the Day Of The Lord

God's nature is to show mercy before judgment. This is why He warns and pleads for people to turn away from sin so they can be raptured out of the worst time the world will ever see. We have learned that Scripture teaches Jesus plans to 'snatch away' His Bride from the holocaust 'Day of the Lord' [Revelation 3:10] which Jeremiah terms the 'Day of Vengeance'. Indeed, it will be payday when God settles with sinners and cleanses the planet a second time with fire unlike the Noahic flood when God used water.

Jeremiah 46:10

10 For this is the **day of the Lord** God of hosts, a **day of vengeance**, that he may avenge him of his adversaries:

and the sword shall devour, and it shall be satiate and made drunk with their blood: for the Lord God of hosts hath a sacrifice in the north country by the river Euphrates.

There are 23 Biblical terms for endtime payday, such as the 'time of Jacob's trouble' [Jeremiah 30:7] and God's 'indignation' [Isaiah 26:20]. They all prophesy of horrific woes involving an extensive fire-bath that will purge the planet of satan's evil cosmos. Jesus' Kingdom will not use anything belonging to satan. The last huge earthquake recorded in the book of Revelation notes that even the mountains will be brought low and islands will vanish away. Every last vestige of the devil's cosmic system will disappear.

The pseudepigraphic book The Wisdom of Sirach or Ecclesiasticus was written after the first temple period when the Hebrews had returned home from their Babylonian captivity. It contains wise sayings, dark speeches, and parables. Because of the wisdom it teaches in confirmation of Old Testament canonical books, I quote a verse from it explaining why people ought to stay watchful and ready for God's final judgment on sin:

Ecclesiasticus 5:7
7 Make no tarrying to turn to the Lord, and put not off from day to day: for suddenly shall the wrath of the Lord come forth, and in thy security thou shalt be destroyed, and perish in the day of vengeance

Notice that the Wisdom of Sirach confirms a sudden cleansing of earth from sin and teaches that men should not tarry nor put off repentance from having strayed away from the Lord. The above quote suggests that commencement of the Day of Vengeance and Rapture are imminent events that usher forth seemingly simultaneously. I will address the prospect of simultaneity in a following chapter. Both events ensnare earth dwellers who think they are living securely along with unprepared Christians hoping for rapture.

Rapturites who have prepared themselves for their wedding to Jesus will quickly in a lightning-like radiation blast be caught up to meet the Lord in the air and will miss the worse time the world will ever experience according to Jesus and Prophet Daniel. Unprepared hopefuls wanting to make Jesus' Bridehood will be left on earth to endure the Day of Vengeance. Like it or not, there are only two options – to be raptured out of the hour of Tribulation, or to remain behind and experience its desolations.

Is It Departure Or Falling Away?

False teaching about the rapture is the reason Paul wrote 2 Thessalonians. Christians in Thessalonica thought they had missed it. Paul wanted them not to despair thinking that they were undergoing persecution because the rapture had already occurred. He told them it could not be true since they had not departed earth and the man of sin had not appeared. Yes, Christians do experience tribulation while sojourning on earth, but the Bible teaches it will not be anything like what will happen during the great Tribulation years when satan's hour comes and Antichrist rules.

Paul denoted the sequence of events concerning rapture and appearance of the man of sin who rules the New World Order.

2 Thessalonians 2:3

3 Let no man deceive you by any means: for that day shall not come, except there come a falling away **first**, and that man of sin be revealed, the son of perdition;

From the above, it is explicit that first, before the man of sin is revealed, there is a falling away. The Greek for 'falling away' is *apostasia* meaning 'to stand away from'. It is used in the New Testament a number of times for a swift physical removal or departure such as when the Roman soldiers in Acts chapter 21 removed Paul quickly by force in the nick of time from the Israelite mob before they killed him. And the context of the passage we're studying so demands that the word be translated departure because three verses down we read…

2 Thessalonians 2:6-8

6 And now ye know what withholdeth that he might be revealed in his time.

7 For the mystery of iniquity doth already work: only he who now *restrains* will *restrain*, until he be taken out of the way.

8 **And then** shall that Wicked (*one*) be revealed, whom the Lord shall consume with the spirit of his mouth, and shall destroy with the brightness of his coming:

This entire passage in 2 Thessalonians is about rapture and not a falling away from faith. The Greek root word of *apostasia* is *aphistemi* meaning 'to remove' or 'to withdraw'. 12 of the 15 times it is used in the New Testament it is referring to a physical departing not a mental defection. In fact, the 72 Hebrew scholars who translated the Masoretic Old Testament text into Greek translated the Hebrew word for 'took' (the English KJB equivalent) as *apostasia* when referring to Enoch being translated in Genesis 5:24. This confirms that Apostle Paul meant a physical departure or removal of saints when he wrote about the falling away of the church in 2 Thessalonians 2:3.

All church fathers and the ten or so Bibles that precursor the 1611 King James Bible used departure to translate *apostasia*. More could be said in support of a departure but space does not permit.

Before leaving this passage note that there is something hindering the appearance of the Antichrist. Paul tells us that the departure or rapture must occur **first** so that the hindering force preventing his appearance and subsequent rule is gone. The force impeding his manifestation is the myriad of Holy-Spirit-filled believers in Christ. Jesus said that hell would not prevail against His church and truly, it has not.

But, when we are gone, there is no more church. Christians left behind will be those believers who did not heed the warning to stay prepared for rapture at any time. After our exodus, the times of the gentiles will be over [Luke 21:24], and God will once again work His will through the nation of Israel. Before the Kingdom Age can emerge, however, the Jews must go through labor pains, i.e., the Tribulational era.

Can Posttribulationalism Comfort?

Posttribulationalism teaches that the rapture will occur at the end of the Tribulation. Given that between ½ to ¾ of the world's population will be killed in that 7-year period according to the book of Revelation, the chances of surviving to be raptured at its end are not good.

If one holds to the Postribulational error that Christians must go through some of the Tribulation, how can one be confident he will not experience God's wrath? After explaining about the rapture in 1 Thessalonians 4:15-18, knowledge which Paul was given by the Lord Himself [4:15], Paul expressly said to *...comfort one another with these words* [4:18]. What words? The words Paul wrote in his letter to Thessaly about Jesus' descent from heaven to seize His Bride off earth so that the man of sin can be revealed [2 Thessalonians 2:6-8]. As mentioned before, Jesus taught Paul that born-again believers indwelt by the Holy Spirit are restraining the evil one from appearing [2 Thessalonians 2:6, 7].

Moreover, Paul tells the Thessalonians to *...wait for his Son from heaven, whom he raised from the dead, even Jesus, which DELIVERED US FROM THE WRATH TO COME* [1 Thessalonians 1:10]. From what wrath are we delivered? We are delivered from the day of the Lord's vengeance at the end of the age when sinners will be judged and found guilty of having transgressed God's holy sovereignty. Their condemnation is to experience the horrific years of the Tribulation period as spelled out in the book of Revelation. Apostle Paul reassures believers, however, that believers *...are not appointed to wrath but to obtain salvation* [1 Thessalonians 5:9].

Some people teach that God's wrath only constitutes the catastrophic and damning bowl or vial judgments at the very end of Tribulation [Revelation 16:1ff], and therefore, believers are raptured right before they occur. This cannot be the case since Jesus cautioned the elect to flee to the mountains to escape the tormenting purge of the lawless one when the abomination of desolation is set up in the temple at midtrib [Matthew 24:15; Mark 13:14].

This event marked out by the books of Daniel and Revelation happens half way through the 2520 prophetic days of Israel's prophetic Sacred Calendar which begins with the spring equinox. Jesus said from that point on there would be great Tribulation such as has not been seen before, and if God did not supernaturally shorten the days, no flesh would be saved. So, for 3½ years great suffering ensues.

In support of Jesus' words in Matthew and Mark, we know from the book of Daniel that God's indignation lasts 7 years since it is the last week of Daniel's 70 Weeks Prophecy in chapter 9:24-27. Therefore, if it is a whole week of years, God's vengeance against sin covers the whole time of 2520 days. Interestingly, 2520 is God's perfect number, and the only number that can be divided evenly by every ordinal 1 to 9. Poetically, God makes a *perfect* end to sin as He executes and *perfects* His justice and judgment in a *perfect* period of days in which He *perfects* His nation and saints!

Hebrews 10:14
14 For by one offering (*on the cross of Calvary*) he (*Jesus*) hath perfected for ever them that are sanctified.

Jewish Jesus Patterns His Marriage after Jewish Weddings

Considering that we are already experiencing the *'beginning of sorrows'* portion of the endtime final days [Matthew 24:8], vigilance to keep ourselves ready for rapture is all the more critical because as I have said repeatedly, when the rapture occurs in the *'twinkling of an eye'*, there will be no time to be getting ready.

Jewish wedding protocols pattern a believer's wedding to Jesus in heaven. The ten virgin parable tells us that Jesus comes for His bride at midnight, and she better be ready lest He leave without her as the foolish virgins found out.[1] Note the agony of unpreparedness in Solomon's Song...

Song of Solomon 5:2-3
2 I sleep, but my heart waketh: it is **the voice of my beloved that knocketh, saying, Open to me**, my sister, my love, my dove, my undefiled: for my head is filled with dew, and my locks with the drops of the night.

3 I have put off my coat; how shall I put it on? I have washed my feet; how shall I defile them?

In verse 3, the Shulamite lover contemplates having already taken care of the worldly activity related to getting ready for bed and hesitates to open the door. She ponders whether she would have to go through the routine ritual of cleansing herself again. To her shock, *hesitation* cost her the privilege of becoming a costly pearl [Matthew 13:46], the king's queen. Read how her belatedness (*hesitation*) to arise from bed cost her greatly:

Song of Solomon 5:6-7
6 I opened to my beloved; but **my beloved had withdrawn himself, and was gone**: my soul failed when he spake: **I sought him, but I could not find him; I called him, but he gave me no answer.**

7 The watchmen that went about the city found me, they smote me, they wounded me; the keepers of the walls took away my veil from me.

---

[1] If a bride betrothed to a Jewish man was not ready at the midnight hour when he came to get her to take her to his home to consummate the marriage, the bridegroom would leave without her. This was actual Jewish protocol in olden times in Israel.

Hesitation is double mindedness, halting between two opinions. Scripture calls it impurity, for Apostle James tells us that believers must purify their hearts of double mindedness since a double minded person is unstable in all his ways [James 1:8]. He further emphasizes in chapter four verse eight that purifying the mind of double mindedness helps to cleanse our hands of sinning.

Apostle John agrees with James because he said that to purify ourselves will make us ready to meet the Savior when He comes back for us [1 John 3:3]. Is the Bible teaching that if we live with one foot in the world (carnal mindedness) and one in the spirit realm (heavenly mindedness), we might not make the rapture? Is it possible there is no gray realm with God? Since the Shulamite woman did not open immediately, her espousal went away without her. Can you see how important it is to be wholly committed and ready for rapture? This book is written to help you not halt between the opinions of whether or not there will be a rapture.

How greatly the Shulamite's woes echo the price the foolish virgins had to pay in Christ's parable of the ten virgins. Not being prepared meant the foolish virgins had to go out into the night to find the necessary oil to light their candles to become a true Bride of Christ. This is similar to the king's beloved in the Song of Solomon rushing out into the darkness to try and find her lover so as not to miss marriage to him. It's unsafe and perilous to miss the rapture.

Look what happened. The night represents the Tribulational darkness in both illustrations. The Shulamite virgin in Song of Solomon ended up being harmed, beaten and ravished as inferred by the stripping away of her veil from her.

Zechariah confirms it will be extremely dangerous in the time of Jacob's trouble [Jeremiah 30:7].

Zechariah 14:2
2 For I will gather all nations against Jerusalem to battle; and the city shall be taken, and the houses rifled, and the women ravished; and half of the city shall go forth into captivity, and the residue of the people shall not be cut off from the city.

Back at the Wedding...

After meeting Jesus in the air, He will take His Bride to His home in heaven where He has built a dwelling place for her [John 14:1-4]. Prior to and in preparation for the consummation of betrothal, at the Bema Seat of Christ, believers will be rewarded for their good deeds. It is at that time they will be arrayed in white linen gowns reflecting their righteous acts [Revelation 19:8]. To confirm the fact that payday is at the rapture, note the closing statement of Jesus in His Apocalyptic revelation:

Revelation 22:12
12 And, behold, I come quickly; and <u>my reward is with me</u>, to give every man according as his work shall be.

Given that this verse is the tenth verse from the end of the entire Bible, is it not significant that Jesus reemphasizes before closing His magnanimous Logos proclamation called the Bible aka the Word of God that He comes quickly? His very last words were *Behold, I come quickly* [Revelation 22:20]. Why did He not say soon? I suggest it is for clarification and warning not to forget the suddenness of His return.

Quickly connotes rapidity, speed, and immediacy, such as highly energized blasts of lightning whereas 'soon' inherently signifies some extent of delay, such as 'after a short time'. Thus, Jesus wants readers never to forget that His return will happen in a moment of time as the flash of a lightening bolt, will be irreversible, and when it does occur, resurrected believers and rapturites will be rewarded immediately at the Bema Seat in heaven while the Tribulation is going on down below on earth. These last words of Jesus in His Book should give pause for contemplation for anyone who wants to be raptured to heaven.

A Jewish wedding lasts for 7 days at the home the bridegroom built for his bride corresponding to the 7-year Tribulation period on earth. (See Numbers 14:34 and Ezekiel 4:6 confirming the day=year Hebraic code.) Then, after the consummation, the groom takes His beautiful bride back to her home to present her in all her magnificent glory to the guests awaiting the marriage supper of the Lamb which takes place at the Bride's home on earth.

After meeting the Lord in the air and proceeding on into heaven, the door is shut [Matthew 25:10] and the wedding nuptials occur. Being a private matter, consummation of the marriage happens in heaven, but the marriage banquet occurs on earth because it is a public affair with invited guests. Guests are Old Testament and Tribulational saints including martyred church believers who did not make the raptured Bridehood [Revelation 7:13, 14].

After tying the knot in heaven, Jesus will bedeck His Bride with jewels to adorn her wedding gown [Isaiah 61:10] before she comes back with Him and the angels [2 Thessalonians 2:7] to vanquish satan [Revelation 19:14]. If as some teach there is no rapture, how can all the parables and mysteries about the

Church Age be true? If even one teaching is untrue, how can we be sure that others like the promise of Eternal Life are not true as well? We can't.

Can you see the disparaging light that compromised teaching causes? To suggest that believers should stay away from prophecy because it is too confusing, which many church leaders are doing, is to negate its equal authority with all other doctrines in the Bible. We must study the whole counsel of God to understand accurately God's plan for humanity.

The reason God gave prophecy in ancient times was to point to who the Messiah would be. Up to 50% of the Old Testament is prophetic pointing to God's righteous servant bringing salvation. Everyone in Jesus' day was looking for the Messiah because they were familiar with the Old Testament books as well as Enoch, Yasher, and the Testaments of the Patriarchs. They knew that the prophecies of those books indicated that the time of the Messiah's visitation was at hand. The person who fulfilled the prophecies in those scrolls is Him. That is why the writers of the New Testament kept saying Jesus fulfilled this or that which was written.

It is reported that Jesus fulfilled some 300 prophecies at His First Advent, and He will fulfill eight times as many at His Second Advent. Given that a third of Scripture is prophetic, and given that prophecy is for edification, exhortation, and comfort, we would be throwing out an awful lot of comfort, hope, and assurance if we heeded spiritual error and avoided prophecy.

Jesus' Promise to Keep His Bride from the Tribulation

Perhaps one of the strongest Scripture verses that reveals the fact that there will be rapture prior to the Tribulation is the following...

Revelation 3:10
10 Because thou hast kept the word of my patience, **I also will keep thee from the hour of temptation,** which shall come upon all the world, to try them that dwell upon the earth.

Greek and Hebrew languages do not have an indefinite article 'a', but they do have a particular article 'the'. Whenever the King James has 'a' or 'an' before a word, check to see if it should be there. When the Greek definite article 'the' precedes a word, it is to emphasize the word and make it emphatic. Otherwise, Greek semantics omits the article before nouns.

In the above verse, note that 'the' precedes 'hour' but not 'temptation'. The Greek text, however, uses the definite article before 'temptation' (testing) <u>and</u> before 'hour' indicating a particular hour and a particular testing of earthdwellers. It should read ...**_the_** hour of **_the_** temptation... Thus, the Greek signifies that hour and temptation are separate emphatic concepts. Therefore, Jesus is impressing upon readers that this will be a particular space of time (the hour) with extremely consequential events (the testing).

In like manner, the King James Bible <u>mistakingly</u> inserts 'a' in front of 'falling away' in 2 Thessalonians 2:3. Again, there is no Greek <u>in</u>definite article. The Greek reads <u>'the</u> _apostasia_' meaning <u>'the</u> falling away' departure implying _a particular_

<u>*departing*</u>. Both Thessaly letters talks about saints departing earth, not about a general malaise of believers moving away from faith.

Because the Tribulation will have repercussions affecting all people, believers as well as unbelievers [Revelation 3:10; 13:6, 14; 14:6], our Lord wants us to know that there is a way to escape this troublesome era. When He says He will keep us 'from' this hour, the Greek word *ek* means 'out of' and 'away from'. How comforting for people hopeful of missing the worst time the world will ever see. Jesus is going to take believing rapturites out of this period that will test people's allegiance to God. Take heart precious brethren; you and I are not going to be here.

Can Jesus do any more than die? He has given us His promise to come get us and take us to where He is [John 14:1-4]. Being well documented in prophetic Scripture, we ought not bury our heads in the sand and ignore the warning to stay prepared for our Lord's return. How does one become ...*worthy to escape* as Luke 21:36 exhorts?

1 John 3:2-3

2 Beloved, now are we the sons of God, and it doth not yet appear what we shall be: but we know that, when he shall appear, we shall be like him; for we shall see him as he is.

3 And every man that hath this hope (*of rapture*) in him <u>purifieth himself</u>, even as (*our Lord*) is pure.

In the above Scripture, Apostle John exhorts believers to live in anticipation of seeing Jesus. But he also advises not to become slack in keeping oneself pure because to be like Him when we see him at our gathering requires purity. Since we do not know when He is coming, we must stay constantly cleansed and holy. Is it possible that a lot of the sinful worldly junk in our lives is because we do not live in anticipation of seeing Him?

Most Christians think that there is plenty of time to get their act together, but is there? Don't count on it. Recall that Sirach's wisdom counsels not to tarry in turning to the Lord. Foolishness thinks there is plenty of time. There isn't if the Lord comes suddenly. Nothing has to be fulfilled before the rapture can occur. It is not like the Second Advent at the end of the Tribulation where according to Scripture numerous things must happen before He comes back. The abomination of desolation must stand in the temple midway in the Tribulation, and there are a multiplicity of woes listed in the book of Revelation that must transpire.

Numerous Scriptures admonish us to watch and be ready. Why would Jesus say it repeatedly in His teachings if it were not important? Watching is not an option nor is it a passive act. Rather it is being spiritually alert that Jesus could come at any moment. This is called imminency in theology and documents that a space of time separates the rapture and Jesus' Second Advent to Mount Olive to end the Armageddon campaign. This means Jesus comes twice, in two phases – at the beginning and again at the end of Daniel's 70th week of his prophecy concerning the Age of Israel.

In the first phase of His return, Jesus comes for His Bride in the air, and the second phase happens 7 years later when He sets foot on terra firma. Scripture reveals at least 14 dissimilarities between the two phases of His returning to earth. Space delimits noting them here, but the Internet is replete with Biblical confirmation. Can you see why prophetic teaching is needed? Without it, we would not have an urgency to be ready at all times because to be caught in the Tribulation will not only be embarrassing but deadly.

Revelation 16:15

15 Behold, I come as a thief. Blessed is he that watcheth, and keepeth his garments, lest he walk naked, and they see his shame. *[Naked implies the absence of a robe of righteousness that's required to enter the heavenly gates.]*

Most sheep in Christian congregations go to church to hear how to better their lifestyle and fulfill ambitions, how to enlarge their personal kingdom on earth. Since the Bible teaches there's nothing good of the flesh [Romans 7:18] nor of the world [James 4:4], wouldn't it be better to learn how to be holy so as not to let our garments become spotted by the world? People need to hear often that our hope is not in this life but in the next one. Exhortation to stay rapture-ready and store up treasure in heaven is the true holiness doctrine that will make a person worthy to escape the coming seals, trumpets, and bowl judgments John wrote about in his prophetic Apocalypse.

Considering the lack of awareness about the ominous state of the world, church services that primarily comfort the afflicted probably should reverse the focus and afflict the comforted. Too many Christians are oblivious to the approaching storm. Jesus must have had a reason to have said that people's hearts would be failing them for fear of those things coming on the earth [Luke 21:26].

The current drift of religion to merge into one monolithic system for the sake of peace and safety is a real problem impeding purity. Ecumenism promoted by the Vatican is not the answer to what is coming. The several recent pandemics and tensions in the Middle East have the world on edge and on verge of WWIII.

Christians need to be encouraged to keep their eyes on the Lord as their source of deliverance from perishing in the upcoming Tribulational turmoil. How can one prepare, though, without the guidance of prophecy? There is too much worldly distraction taking people's eyes off the important things in life thanks to technology.

Satan does not want us to live in the light of our Lord's soon return, so he gets people involved in anything that distracts from spending time in the Word with Jesus. For example, the myriad of learning curves associated with smart phones and Internet technology is probably satan's top stealth weaponry blinding one's eternality.

The Lord's return is not a reality with the majority of Christians. Don't let the cares of this life, the uncertainty of riches, or the lust of other things choke the Word so that it becomes unfruitful to you [Mark 4:19]. We are in the harvest season of the Church Age, so I suggest you use your sickle and reap the souls around you that are languishing for want of truth.

CHAPTER -2

How Critical Is The Rapture Doctrine?

The Lord has said it over and over, *...take head to yourselves ...lest that day come upon you unawares* (Luke :21:34). The enemy is out there seeking whom he may devour. He does not want you to get into prophecy and find out about the times we are in. He does not want you to live in the light of our Lord's soon return and our imminent departure to go be where He is (Luke : 14: 1-3).

Given that the rapture happens in *the twinkling of an eye*, in a moment of time, [1 Corinthians 15:52] means there will be no time to be getting ready when He shows up. You must do it now for Jesus indicated He is coming as a lightning bolt for people eager to see Him. He is not coming for a half-hearted Bride.

Some Bible teachers even say that refusing to repent now while heaven's door is still open puts backsliders and foot draggers at risk of going to hell. They note that Scripture says unrepentant people who love not the truth about holiness preparation for rapture will be left behind because they were deceived into rejecting the rapture doctrine. Not loving truth opens one up to strong delusion to believe the lie that will propel the Antichrist to power.

2 Thessalonians 2:8-12

8 And then shall that Wicked (one, the Antichrist) be revealed, whom the Lord shall consume with the spirit of his mouth, and shall destroy with the brightness of his coming:

9 Even him, whose coming is after the working of Satan with all power and signs and lying wonders,

10 And with all deceivableness of unrighteousness in them that perish; because they received not the love of the truth, that they might be saved.

11 And FOR THIS CAUSE God shall send them strong delusion, that they should believe a lie:

12 That they all might be damned who believed not the truth, but had pleasure in unrighteousness.

Paul's prognosis above about people being duped and damned for not loving the truth, for not studying the Word to find its wisdom and counsel, was a part of the mystery doctrine of the rapture that Jesus gave him [1 Thessalonians 4:15]. Loving truth is loving Jesus since He said He is the way, the truth, and the life [John 14:6]. Therefore, loving Jesus is loving the Word of God because the Bible proclaims Him to be the Word of God in Revelation 19:20.

As you can see from what Paul said, it is dangerous to ignore end time truth because disinterest can cause a person not to prepare and hence miss becoming part of the rapture Bride. I suggest you deepen your faith in the doctrine about our departure so as not to be lured into the counterfeit teaching that there will be none or be belated in the Tribulation. Remember that Enoch was translated that he should not see death by his faith in God's spoken word regarding the subject.

Hebrews 11:5

5 <u>By faith</u> Enoch was translated that he should not see death; and was not found, because God had translated him: for before his translation he had this testimony, that he pleased God.

How do we please God? By believing in rapture as Enoch did we please God. Given opportunity to respond to truth and rejecting it is tantamount, say some, to rejecting God's offer of salvation, of deliverance, of healing, of preservation, and even of being raptured. Rather than argue the point to be raptured or not, it is the better part of wisdom just to do what the Scripture says and prepare for takeoff. Why would anyone opt for going through the Tribulation chancing being supernaturally protected as some Bible teachers teach?

The Tragic Consequence of Rejecting Truth

Matthew 7:21-23

21 Not every one that saith unto me, Lord, Lord, shall enter into the kingdom of heaven; but he that doeth the will of my Father which is in heaven.

22 <u>MANY</u> will say to me in that day, Lord, Lord, have we not prophesied in thy name? and in thy name have cast out devils? and in thy name done many wonderful works?

23 And then will I profess unto them, <u>I never knew you</u>: depart from me, ye that work iniquity.

Notice that Jesus did not say few nor did He say some. He said many. The word implies the majority. He did not say I knew you once but you lost it. He said "I never knew you". These are some of the most serious words in the Bible. They imply that the majority of Christians have never <u>wholly</u> committed their lives to Christ. Hence, they have never studied the whole counsel of God.

Compare this judgment of Jesus with what He said to the five virgins who were not ready for the Bridegroom's coming to consummate the marriage. The half-committed betrothed-ones revealed their lack of eagerness to stay prepared for the Lord's return because they did not provide extra oil with which to meet the Bridegroom.

Jesus said He will tell them, "I know you not". This indicates these rapture hopefuls never developed an intimate relationship with the Lord. 'Knowing' in Scripture is often used euphemistically for intimacy via intercourse between a man and woman. Hence, Jesus is implying that during His absence His Bride will be busy learning about the intimacies that flow out of a husband-wife covenantal commitment.

Some people think that all you have to do to be saved is to say you believe in Jesus Christ. Demons acknowledge Jesus is the Christ but they are doomed forever. Easy believism will not get a person to heaven. Why? It is because even though salvation is simple – having sincere faith in the gospel of Jesus as little children have in the words of their parents – maintaining salvation is testy.

Billy Graham, the foremost evangelist of the 20th century said that 90% or more of his converts backslid and never followed up with a real commitment to Christ. Jesus is not coming for a half-committed Bride which is the reason we need to purify our hearts and stop mixing Christian dogma with other religions' faith practices.

Revelation 5:9-10

9 And they sung a new song, saying, Thou art worthy to take the book, and to open the seals thereof: for thou wast slain, and hast redeemed US to God by thy blood out of every kindred, and tongue, and people, and nation;

10 And hast made US unto our God kings and priests: and WE shall reign on the earth.

One of the most convincing arguments in support of a Pretribulational rapture is found in the above two verses taken from the Apocalypse.   It is urgent that you understand Posttribulationists say that the church will experience all of the Tribulation and Prewrath people say that the church experiences 3/4th or more of it since Prewrath people theorize that rapture occurs just prior to the endtime bowl judgments.

Scholars agree that chapters 4 and 5 of Revelation are heavenly scenes depicting Jesus claiming title deed to earth. They are prologue to the devastations outlined in chapters 6 through 19 wherein are delineated God's judgmental wrath against sin.

I believe that the seals of chapter 6 represent a Table of Contents of things to come upon earth during the 7-year Tribulation.   They are the Apocalypse book's 'forward' explaining, as all forwards do, what the reader will learn as he or she reads the book. In that respect, I submit that the seals are not progressive events as most teachers teach, but stand-alone concepts that disclose disasters and devastations resulting from a sin-sick world, and they will occur simultaneously off-and-on throughout the era.

Before the Lion of the tribe of Judah aka Jesus actually opens the deed and removes the seals one by one, the 24 elders sing a song to Him rejoicing because they are worthy to have become a part of the marriage to the Lamb. Who are these elders? Are they the raptured church ending the Church Age, or, are they martyred Tribulational saints? That is our quest.

In the song, the first person plural pronouns 'us' and 'we' as highlighted above refer to the ones singing the song. Hence, the redeemed singers watching the ceremony before the throne of God are the referents of the pronouns in verses 9 and 10. They are already standing before the throne of God, before the opening of seal 5 in chapter 6 of the title deed which speaks to the martyrs of the period. Since they precede the Tribulational accounts of chapters 6 through 19, how could they be martyrs from it? The events of the era have not yet started.

Having been redeemed, and having been made kings and priests according to Revelation 1:6 and 5:10, the singers in my opinion depict the raptured body of Christ. They are ecstatic to be present to observe the Lamb's assumption of God's 'Avenger of Blood', a blood covenant practice whereby a kinsman revenges the integrity of a dishonored brother. Jesus wars against disobedient sinners who reject God's free offer of salvation through His Son's magnanimous work of the cross. How ignoble to disrespect the gracious blood of Calvary.

But a controversy of late has arisen whereby rapture naysayers teach that the 'us' is a mistranslation and should read 'them' making the statements refer to people who will die during the Tribulation.

Here's The Problem

Jesus said that in the mouth of two witnesses let a matter be established. So let me give you two witnesses that prove the point that these redeemed singers represent the raptured church and not Tribulational converts.

Some 83 times the Bible speaks in the New Testament about saved believers being 'in Christ'. This is a technical phrase Paul uses mostly, although Peter likes it too, referring to Church Age believers who have been baptized into the body of Christ [Galatians 3:26-28]. Since Jesus comes to get His body at the rapture, the redeemed songsters are the believers who purified and sanctified themselves so as to make rapture at the end of the seven church eras of Revelation Chapter 3.

When Jesus said to John in Revelation 4:1, *'Come up hither',* Apostle John depicted the church being caught up or raptured to heaven. And it happens **before** the scroll is given to Jesus to open in chapter 5, **before** the Tribulation starts. Thus, they are Church Age believers and hence Pretribbers.

Witness #1

I have read that a most respected Bible teacher who holds to the Postribulational rapture stance, has said that if the pronouns are 'us' and 'we' in the above verses, the redeemed people referred to in the verses are singing about their own redemption and must refer to the church. He asserts that if true, the two verses immediately make us all Pretribulational, and we will not be on earth during the worst time the world will ever see. Let's see if this opinion is correct and thus self-condemning.

This assertion of a prominent Posttrib promoter who contends that the rapture occurs at the very end of the

Tribulation amidst the battle of Armageddon contradicts Posttribulationism. According to Posttrib theory, like a yoyo raptured believers go up to meet the Lord in the air and come right back down with Him to reign on earth.

Various commentaries scoff at Pretribulationalists who use this passage in Revelation as proof that the church will not be on earth during God's holy wrath against sin. Why would anyone want to follow people who promote teachings which can hinder faith to escape through rapture multiplied catastrophes and horrendous woes as delineated in the book of Revelation? Since it takes faith to obtain any blessing from God, the magnitude of the error in judgment is huge.

Most translations of the Bible have footnotes explaining that the 'us' should be translated 'them'. Some translations spuriously insert words like 'men' (New International Version) and 'people' (The Living Bible) for the pesky pronouns. Furthermore, many footnotes also say that most ancient manuscripts use 'them'. Even a few publishers of the uncopyrighted KJV has that footnote. Precious reader, **footnotes are not facts**.

One Bible scholar who holds three Ph.D. degrees and teaches ancient history did a search on the footnote comment. He searched all the existent Greek manuscripts of New Testament texts of which there are over 5,000 and found that there are only 95 extant Greek manuscripts about the book of Revelation. Many of these are only fragments.

Of the 95 available old manuscripts he reports that only 24 have these two verses of chapter 5. Here is his critical discovery. 23 of the 24 extant manuscripts read 'us' in verse 9. The only one that says 'them' is the Codex Alexandrinus text birthed in Alexandria Egypt, which is known to contain compilations of Gnostic teachings of Philo (a Jewish scholar who was a lover of Plato) mixed with Hebrew doctrine. What contamination causing confusion!

It was also discovered that even the Catholic Latin Vulgate reads 'us' in both verses in conformity with the KJV. Later versions of the 1611 KJV read 'us' as well. All other ethnic Bibles translated from Greek into the particular language of ethnicity such as the Coptic, Syriac, Peshitta, et al, all read 'us' too. Consequently, we can safely say that the 'us' is referring to the redeemed 24 elders who represent the raptured church praising and worshipping God in heaven while the Tribulation is going on down below.

Everywhere Paul and the other apostles and missionaries went, they appointed elders to oversee the flocks of God. A search of the New Testament will show that 'elder' was the universal term used for church leaders. Hence, the 24 elders is merely a representative number of the entire group of raptured people.

In the Old Testament, teachers of the people were priests. In chapter 24 of the book of First Chronicles, we find King David ordering the priestly caste into 24 groups, and in chapter 25 he ordered the temple singers into groups of 24. So, the number 24 appears to be a number representative of groups of God's people.

Revelation 4:4

4 And round about the throne (*thronou*) were four and twenty <u>seats</u> (*thronous*): and upon the <u>seats</u> I saw four and twenty elders sitting, clothed in <u>white raiment</u>; and they had on their heads <u>crowns</u> of gold.

The word translated 'seats' in the above upon which the elders sit is the Greek word for throne. It is the same word for God's throne in this same verse. So we see that the elders were sitting on **thrones**, clothed in **white raiment** and sporting **crowns**. These three items identify who the elders are because we find Jesus using these terms to refer to overcomers in His dissertation about the 7 churches representing church ages in chapter 2 and 3 of Revelation.

He told the Smyrna overcomers they would receive a <u>crown</u> of life [Revelation 2:10]; the overcomers in Sardis would be clothed in <u>white raiment</u> [Revelation 3:5]; and the overcomers in Laodicea would be granted privilege to sit on Jesus' <u>throne</u> [Revelation 3:21]. Wouldn't you say this is compelling evidence documenting who the elders are in chapters 4 and 5 of Revelation?

Witness #2

The second witness is a proponent of the Prewrath position whose well-written book caused a stir in the churches some 25 years ago. Without detailing why he proposes that the church will experience all but the last Tribulational bowl judgments, let me cut to the chase and give you his own commentary about the cited verses above regarding the pronoun usage.

In his book, he comments that his whole doctrinal Prewrath stance hinges on who the redeemed are in chapter 5 verses 9 and 10 of the Revelation given to John. He says that if they are indeed **singing about themselves and <u>not people saved during</u> the Tribulation**, his entire thesis regarding the Prewrath position falls apart! Think about that. Given the truth documented above concerning ancient texts, his Prewrath assertion testifies that his whole book is a waste of time to read.

Considering that internal Scriptural evidence and language syntax shows the 24 elders are singing about themselves, and considering that only one of the 5,000+ existing ancient texts support using 'they' instead of 'us' in verse nine, I submit that people quit spending time straddling the fence of double mindedness, which is impurity of mind [James 4:8]. Since time is of essence and rapture could happen at any moment, obey the Lord and watch for His imminent return as Paul and the Ante Nicene early church fathers did.

It is important that we study prophecy because it is through prophetic utterances of old-timers from Adam to Malachi that we know Jesus is the prophesied Messiah Whom God said He would send to save humanity from eternal death. Has not our study of these two pivotal verses of Scripture not answered why prophecy is necessary? I believe they clearly show the reason we are admonished to study the Bible in order to rightly divide the Word of Truth [2 Timothy 2:15].

We would be wise to heed what Enoch said about prophecy in his book which he gave to Noah. Enoch as well as The School of the Prophets initiated by Elijah taught that it was a sin not to study prophecy. What a tremendous heavy-weight warning from God's spokes-persons for anyone but especially for church leaders who dodge teaching prophecy. Do they dodge it because they do not understand it and do not want to rock the boat floating their financial stability, or, because after enlightenment, they might have to admit having allied with sacred-cow errors?

Nevertheless, prophecy cannot be understood correctly without rightly dividing the Word of Truth and that takes study [2 Timothy 2:15]. First and foremost, Christians need to continually renew their minds through meditating Scripture to learn God's methods of doing things which is Biblical wisdom. After the mind is cleansed of worldly wisdom through Bible study, prophecy will naturally fall into place. But without Biblical wisdom, it is impossible to discern when false teachers and prophets are seducing you.

Foundational knowledge regarding the person of Jesus and His work on the cross is imperative if you want to walk in power with the Lord. It is described in Isaiah chapter 53 and explained in the letters of Paul to the Ephesians and Colossians. If you will dwell in these places of Scripture, heavily meditated in them, you will be able to access all the privileges of your great inheritance through Jesus and to release power to overcome satan, sin, sickness, and lack. But, it takes faith to access what one needs. So, along with studying prophecy, my advice is to learn all you can about faith, how to use it like a tool, and why it is necessary to please God [Hebrews 11:6].

PROLOGUE TO THE KINGDOM AGE

Luke 21:36

Watch ye therefore, and pray always, that ye may be accounted worthy to escape all these things that shall come to pass, and to stand before the Son of man.

The Lord spoke the above words of Scripture when He gave the Olivet Discourse[1] to His disciples. We do not have space to inspect the whole discourse; but the verse above is germane to understanding that the rapture precedes the Tribulational era of time. Therefore, we will examine it closely.

On the Mount of Olives, the words of Luke 21:36 summarized Jesus' teaching concerning things that would come to pass related to the Temple's destruction and the cleansing of earth preceding the setting up of His Kingdom. When He admonished His followers to *pray always*, He was advising them to stay alert, sin free, and prayed up by praying with the frequency of a hacking cough.

---

[1] The Olivet Discourse is Jesus' answer to His disciples' question about when the Temple would be destroyed. It is recorded in Matthew 24, Mark 13, and Luke 21.

Notice why He said it is critical to watch and pray, *...that ye may be <u>accounted worthy to **ESCAPE**</u> all these things that shall come to pass* in the day that God's wrath will be poured out upon sin. Jesus implied it will be so bad during that time that everyone left behind will wish they had escaped from earth in the rapture. Is that not the implication of being escape worthy?

Having explained the rapture in part in the foregoing two chapters, you can easily see it is a manifestly weird, strange, and inexplicable event, a supernatural occurrence that will surprise and shock an unbelieving, unprepared world for the things which will undoubtedly happen. God does not lie, and if Jesus advises people not to fall asleep but to watch and pray always, we best do so.

The things that will happen as per our Lord's prophetic declaration in the 21st chapter of Luke are events and dealings that embody God's judgment on sin. The Bible has much to say about this time just before manifestation of the Kingdom of Heaven. Someone has counted as many as 1800 references in the Old Testament to Christ's rule on earth which is widely heralded as the Kingdom Age. Let me add that 17 of the Old Testament books give prominence to it. In the New Testament, according to one researcher, 23 of the 27 books refer to it and of 216 chapters in the New Testament, there are over 310 references. It is obvious that God does not want us ignorant about His agenda for His creation. Could that be why Paul said 8 times in his letters... *I would not have you ignorant brethren?*

Background: The Indignation of God

In the First Testament of the Bible, the word 'indignation' is used consistently for God's wrath on sin. So, let's let the Bible define the word. Psalms 69:24 reads, *Pour out thine **indignation** upon them, <u>and</u> let thy **wrathful anger** take hold of them*. This agrees with Strong's Hebrew Lexicon defining 'indignation' as fury, anger, or rage, especially God's displeasure against sin. The Hebrew noun comes from a root word meaning to foam at the mouth signifying raging madness as a dog with rabies or grotesque behavior displayed by possessed individuals in whom a demon manifests.

Indignation, therefore, means outrage so intense it erupts in violent behavior, and from the Psalmist's doubling of two words connoting rage – *wrathful anger* – we can assume indignation means the extreme fury of God in action. Could that be the reason Jesus implied escaping that time is a blessing only worthy people will experience?

The Lord is patient, compassionate, and mercifully gracious, which is why the whole world has not been judged for its sin for several millennia. We know from Scripture that God, as the supreme Judge of all things, does not personally decree punishment until iniquity is full which can take hundreds and even thousands of years [Genesis 15:16].

Scripture teaches that Abraham's descendants could not take over Canaan until the fourth generation, 400 years after God promised it to Abraham, because *...the iniquity of the Amorites was not yet full* [Genesis 15:16]. But when it reaches a limit that God alone decides, He will act to preserve His holy creation from self-destruction and to accomplish His will.

We have record of God's displeasure over sin when He personally intruded in the cosmos to eliminate several severely sin-infested cities, of which Sodom and Gomorrah were two [Genesis 19:24]; and we know *He cast upon Egypt the fierceness of his anger, wrath, ...indignation, and trouble, by* permitting satan to send *evil angels among* them to plague them.

He made a way to his anger and *spared not their soul from death, but gave their life over to the pestilence* and permitted *all the firstborn in Egypt to be smitten* by the angel of death [Psalms 78:49]. Just for the record, God does not spoil things Himself. He is not a spoiler. However, by permitting evil angels to destroy, it appears like God does it.[2]

The patience of God reached its limit when He disciplined unrepentant, stiffnecked Israel, His own people, with the Diaspora [Lamentations 4:7]. He removed His hedge of protection about them and permitted satan's host to afflict them through dispersion as slaves to other countries.

God's mercy and forbearance is enormous, but make no mistake about it, God has promised He will not tolerate sin forever. One day He will again release His pent up anger as He did in the flood of Noah, pour out His wrath without reservation, and manifest His righteous indignation on sin. No part of the world will escape. That day is known in Scripture as the Day of the Lord. Sin will be purged by fire the next time God pours out His wrath on sin, and **escaping** God's wrath in the Day of the Lord is what Jesus was alluding to in our opening text.

The Day of the Lord

The term 'Day of the Lord' is used at least 31 times in the Old Testament to refer to the day when God establishes His Kingdom on earth for the thousand-year reign of Christ, David's promised heir who will rule as the Lion of the tribe of Judah [Revelation 5:5]. Some Biblicists believe it includes the preparatory events of the Tribulational seven years. It is the day

---

[2] Robert Young, one of the foremost scholars of Hebrew and Greek has said that because there is no permissive tense in the English language, very often Hebrew permissive verbs were translated into English with the causative tense implying that God Himself destroyed, hurt, or smote men with evil or woeful conditions. In reality, God permits satan to work His will when people will not respond to His warnings. When man gets out from under God's protective covering by his own willful choice to not follow God's instructions, he opens himself up to all kinds of satanic oppression. Therefore, satan is the spoiler, not God.

God prepared before the world began to reestablish the Garden of Eden decrees given to humanity that Adam treasonously turned over to satan.

After 6,000 years, the tyrannical despot demigod Lucifer aka satan who wields power oppressively and is destitute of compassion will be deposed as god of the world [2 Corinthians 4:4]. The true God will finally have His day in court. He will demonstrate righteousness and justice in such a manner that peace, love, and mercy will reign supreme and the whole earth will know the fullness of God's glory [Isaiah 6:3].

The Lion of the Tribe of Judah

Because Jesus is the Lion of Judah who will rule earth with a rod of iron [Psalms 2:9; Revelation 2:27; 12:5; 19:15], He will not permit rebellion against Kingdom laws that are righteous, holy, and protective of all Kingdom citizenry. Note the prophecy Jacob spoke over his son Judah on his deathbed:

> Genesis 49:9, 10
> 9 Judah is a lion's whelp ...
> 10 The <u>sceptre</u> (*a symbol of tribal authority in a nation*) shall not depart from Judah, nor a lawgiver <u>from between his feet</u>, until **Shiloh come,** and unto him shall the <u>gathering of the people be</u>.

Shiloh in Hebrew means 'peacemaker' and refers to the Prince of Peace, the One who makes peace between God and man, the man Christ Jesus. Since Jesus is from the tribe of Judah, He is the Lion in verse nine above. Verse ten confirms that Shiloh comes from Judah; therefore, it is pointing to Jesus as the coming lawgiver from Israel whose scepter shall never depart from His Kingdom.

The above also prophesies that Shiloh's tribal authority will be extended to encompass a peaceful government over all people, Jews and gentiles alike. The scepter of a king nestles between a ruler's feet while sitting on a throne with the end of the scepter's shaft pointing towards himself as he to whom the scepter belongs. Thus, the prophecy predicts that when Shiloh aka Jesus comes, it is 'He to whom it [the Scepter] belongs' or 'He whose right to it is come'.

Shiloh Is the Arbitrator of Peace between God and Man

Note that the book of Revelation confirms the Genesis 49 prophecy pointing to Jesus as Shiloh whose right it is to rule earth.

Revelation 5:5
5 And one of the elders saith unto me, Weep not: behold, <u>the Lion of the tribe of Juda, the Root of David</u>, hath prevailed to open the book, and to loose the seven seals thereof.

In conquering death through resurrection, Jesus through His humanity seized back authority of earth from satan giving Him the right to cleanse earth of his cosmic rule.

Revelation 19:13-16
13 ... Jesus' name is called <u>The Word of God</u>.
14 And the armies which were in heaven followed him upon white horses, clothed in fine linen, white and clean.
15 And out of his mouth goeth a sharp sword, that with it he should smite the nations: and <u>he shall rule them</u>

<u>with a rod of iron</u>: and he treadeth the winepress of the fierceness and wrath of Almighty God.

16 And he hath on his vesture and on his thigh a name written, KING OF KINGS, AND LORD OF LORDS.

During His rule of the Millennial Age, Jesus' words will be rods of iron enforcing justice and judgment without equivocation. Even though people who populate the Millennium will have survived the Tribulation without dying, they will still have Adam's sin nature acquired at their physical birth. Notwithstanding restoration of the Edenic environment in the Millennium, like people today, a spiritual rebirth is necessary as Jesus told Nicodemus in order to enter heaven and to stand before a holy God.

Jesus informed Nicodemus that Eternal Life is dependent upon one's nature, not individual sins. It takes the eternality of the nature of God. i.e., an influx of Eternal Life that only God has, to live forever. Thanks be to God that we believers who are born again are the seed of Christ and heirs of Eternal Life according to the promise given to Abraham [Galatians 3:29]. Because Jesus lives and reigns forever, we too shall live and reign forever.

Psalms 89:35-37

35 Once have I sworn by my holiness that I will not lie unto David.

36 <u>His seed shall endure forever</u>, and his throne as the sun before me.

37 It shall be established for ever as the moon, and as a faithful witness in heaven. Selah.

The Millenniums of Earth

In establishing the visible presence of Jesus' Kingdom which has been hidden in the hearts of men [Luke 17:21] for almost 2,000 years, the first priority of business is to cleanse the earth of sin and wickedness. Being holy and pure, God is not going to use anything in which satan has had a hand.

Wherefore, the Day of the Lord begins with discomfort and progresses into great Tribulation [Matthew 24:21; Revelation 2:22; 7:14]. The process of ridding earth of every vestige of satan's cosmic rule takes seven years and is known as the last week of Daniel's   70-week Prophecy. This prophecy concerns the occurrence in time when the deposed Israeli majestic kingdom of Solomon would be restored.

Because Jesus' Kingdom is prophesied to be the last millennium of God's week of seven millenniums [Revelation 20:2-7], and because there is a seven-year period of cleansing earth before it starts, Biblicists disagree about whether it is the last Shemittah cycle of seven years of the Age of Israel or the beginning one of the Millennium. Regardless of its placement, the Bible declares it to be the time of Israel's labor pains that birth the Kingdom Age [Jeremiah 30:7].

Some Biblicists believe it starts the Millennial Age as an embryonic week of bringing order out of chaos as in the creation. Others see it as the last week of the Age of Israel ending Israel's 490-year time frame for being God's client nation through which He communicates with the world.

Suffice it to say that God is not finished with Israel for Paul reports that *God hath not cast away his people which he foreknew* [Romans 11:2]. She will again emerge as the nation from which the King of Kings will rule for a thousand years. Being Jewish, Jesus will rule from His Jewish nation Israel. At the end of earth's 7,000 decreed years of space-time existence, God will create a new and more glorious heaven and earth that will be eternal [Revelation 21:1].

According to Apostle Peter, there were 7 days of creation, and there will be 7 millenniums (7,000 years) for earth's space-time existence.

2 Peter 3:8
3:8 But, beloved, be not ignorant of this one thing, that <u>one day is with the Lord as a thousand years</u>, and a thousand years as one day.

Therefore, a generation of earth's existence is 1,000 years in conformity with Genesis 2:4's declaration whereby the Spirit implied through Moses that the days of creation correlate with the days of earth's existence: *'These'* (a reference to the 7 days of creation) *be the generations of the heavens and of the earth* [Genesis 2:4]. So, after the seventh millennium, John…

Revelation 21:1
21:1 …<u>saw a new heaven and a new earth</u>: for the first heaven and the first earth were passed away; and there was no more sea.

Bringing Order Out Of Chaos

Apostle John clearly teaches in Revelation that Jesus will rule one thousand years, and if the seven-year week of the Tribulation during which satan rules earth were the first seven years of the 1,000 years, the Antichrist would be ruling during the first years of the Millennium delimiting Christ's reign to 993 years in toto. Six times the Holy Spirit indicated through Apostle John that the rule of Christ would be exactly 1,000 years [Revelation 20:2-7]. It is as if the Spirit through John's Revelation wanted no mistake about it.

The following Old Testament Scriptures indicate that the seven-year period is a dark day of gloom. And since this well-known and distinguished Kingdom begins with pain and anguish as it is birthed into visibility like a baby is birthed through travail, I submit that Daniel's 70th week of the Age of Israel is the womb of the Day of the Lord.

Scriptural Passages Foreboding Trouble

Isaiah 13:6

6 Howl ye; for the day of the Lord is at hand; it shall come as a destruction from the Almighty.

Isaiah 13:9

9 Behold, the day of the Lord cometh, cruel both with wrath and fierce anger, to lay the land desolate: and he shall destroy the sinners thereof out of it.

Jeremiah 46:10

10 For this is the day of the Lord God of hosts, a day of vengeance, that he may avenge him of his adversaries:

Joel 1:15

15 Alas for the day! for the day of the Lord is at hand, and as a destruction from the Almighty shall it come.

Amos 5:18

18 Woe unto you that desire the day of the Lord! to what end is it for you? the day of the Lord is darkness, and not light.

Zephaniah 1:18

18 Neither their silver nor their gold shall be able to deliver them in the day of the Lord 's wrath; but the whole land shall be devoured by the fire of his jealousy: ...

Malachi 4:5

5 Behold, I will send you Elijah the prophet before the coming of the great and dreadful day of the Lord: ...

These are only seven verses of the many prophetic passages saying that the Day of the Lord begins with trouble.

God's method in creating is usually to bring order out of chaos. He started the creation week with *darkness upon the face of the deep* [Genesis 1:2]; and after bringing forth light from the chaotic darkness, He named the first part of each day by its dark division...*The evening and the morning were the first day* [1:5]; and He said the same thing every day thereafter. This is the reason Jewish days begin at sundown instead of midnight.

The Day of the Lord Births the Kingdom Age

God formed the nation of Israel in the dark bowels of a heathen nation and birthed her with great travail as He permitted evil angels to plague Egypt causing her to bring forth God's firstborn [Exodus 4:23]. In like manner, God will birth His Kingdom Age. Evil spirits will plague earth-dwellers with formidable forceps forcing its extraction from the darkness. Through catastrophic upheavals and a reign of terror by Antichrist, the cosmos will unwillingly release its hidden captive. Satan's cosmic system will disintegrate from the powerful birthing judgments of the Lord upon it.

Daniel 2:44
44 ...In the days of these (*gentile) kings* shall the God of heaven set up a kingdom, which shall never be destroyed: and the kingdom shall not be left to other people, but it shall break in pieces and consume all these kingdoms, and it shall stand for ever.

In the days of these kings... is a reference to the time of gentile rule. During this time, the Kingdom of Heaven covertly advances in the hearts of men. It vanished from earth after the first Adam sinned, but God began reestablishing it on earth with the coming of the second Adam, Jesus [1 Corinthians 15:45-47]. As stated in the above Scripture, when God's kingdom bursts forth from the womb of humanity it will crush and consume all the nations comprising satan's kingdom of darkness.

Gentile time for ruling earth began with Nebuchadnezzar, king of Babylon, and it will be completed at the end of the Tribulation. Satan's uncontested authority over earth lasted only until Jesus' First Advent. When Jesus came in the fullness of time [Galatians 4:4] and paid the ransom for earth's redemption [Matthew 20:28], satan lost unchallenged authority upon earth. In rising from death, Jesus took the devil's power of death away from him [Hebrews 12:14, 15].

Having defeated death and satan by paying the price for the planet's redemption, all authority (legal right and unequaled might) in heaven and earth was conferred upon Jesus by God. The Redeemer immediately delegated His authority to His followers [Matthew 28:18, 19] who can bind and loose the devil themselves [Matthew 18:18], an authority Old Testament saints did not have. Given that Christians have power to bind and loose, the body of Christ ought to be chasing the devil to the gates of hell instead of the enemy making casualties out of Christians.

Why Christians have not been able to unseat the devil in many places of the earth is a matter beyond the scope of this paper. Our purpose in this book is to find out what God has envisioned for the last days so we can get in step with His plans, fulfill our purpose in life, and get ready for rapture.

After taking the keys of death away from satan through resurrection [Revelation 1:18], Jesus opened the gates of hell to release its prisoners who were awaiting their Redeemer in the upper region of hell known as Paradise. At the same time, Jesus opened the gates to the Kingdom of Heaven.

Whoever makes Jesus Lord of their lives enters His Kingdom while alive on earth; in fact, one must do so before he or she dies. The day is coming, however, when the gates will be closed as we shall see below. Secluded in the hearts of regenerated people, the Kingdom has been enlarging in the bowels of earth's population. The baby is so big today; she is pressing to be born. When rapture happens, Jacob's trouble will begin.

Jeremiah 30:7
7 Alas! for that day is great, so that none is like it: it is even the time of Jacob's trouble ; but he shall be saved out of it.

The 'trouble' with Jacob is that the prophesied Kingdom is travailing to come forth. The Kingdom's struggle to be released causes severe distress and pain for the womb confining her. Tribulational woes will shatter and crush the nations within which she covertly grew [Daniel 2:44], and her emergence will be the place of her conception – Jerusalem.

Zechariah 12:2-3
2 Behold, I will make Jerusalem a cup of trembling unto all the people round about, when they shall be in the siege both against Judah and against Jerusalem.
3 And in that day will I make Jerusalem a burdensome stone for all people: all that burden themselves with it shall be cut in pieces, though all the people of the earth be gathered together against it.

Jerusalem is the cause of much world militancy today. The constant conflagrations and striving in the Middle East are signs that the baby wants to be born. Once the process starts, it is impossible for a birth mother to say "I don't want this baby. Pains begone!"

Balderdash! Laboring to bring forth a baby persists until it is born. The current Middle East peace negotiations are notwithstanding. Israel's *covenant with death* that she is determined to make with her enemies *shall be annulled and her agreement with hell shall not stand* [Isaiah 28:18].

The Oslo Accords at President Clinton's oversight, the Annapolis Conference at President George Bush's watch, and the Abrahamic Accords at President Donald Trump's headship have all been negotiated in pursuit of peace between Israel and Palestine, but none will protect Israel from the Tribulation that brings forth the Kingdom Age.

Regardless of the peace pact parleyed between Israel and the Palestinians, Kingdom labor pains must last seven years to fulfill Daniel's prophecy of a *'determined'* seventy weeks [Daniel 9:24] before the Davidic Kingdom can be reestablished. Sixty-nine weeks of 490 years have transpired. The last week has been on hold for over 2,000 years. The two millennia of intercalated world history is sort of a 'time out' period which professional sports incorporate in their rules.

Our Lord referred to Daniel's 70 Weeks Prophecy in His account of the last days' scenario. In this 'time out' period it is wise to follow Jesus' advice: ...*when these things* (prophesied endtime events) *begin to come to pass, then look up, and lift up your heads, for your redemption draweth nigh* [Luke 21:28]. Can you feel Jesus' pull on your heart in this day of terrorism with its potential for nuclear attack and worldwide destruction?

The Day of the Lord Comes Upon the Holy and the Unholy

Chapter 1 of this book documented that there will be a rapture of God's saints to heaven [1Thessalonians 4:16, 17]. Accepting this as true, the next important question is when will it happen? I wish I could tell you. If I could, none of us would be unprepared for it. But the Bible explains in several places that the event is going to come as a thief suddenly and swiftly without warning and hence, by surprise. Therefore, we must always be ready.

We learned from Paul's first letter to Thessaly that believers wondered about what was going to happen to loved ones who died before Jesus returned. Would they not participate in the rapture wedding? Paul comforted them with assurance from the Lord Himself that the rapture event would not prevent sleeping loved ones from participation in the marriage of the Lamb. In fact, dead saints will rise to meet Jesus in the air before those alive ascend to meet Him in clouds [1 Thessalonians 4:16, 17].

Since the rapture ushers in the Day of the Lord, no one knows when it will happen because the Day of the Lord comes suddenly as a thief [verse 2 below]. False teachers had troubled them with misleading and frightening thoughts that the Day of the Lord had come due to growing persecution in Rome's empire. They were lied to about having missed the rapture. Paul assuaged their fear in a second letter; but let's look at what he told them in his first letter.

1 Thessalonians 5:1-9

1 But of the times and the seasons, brethren, ye have no need that I write unto you.

2 For yourselves know perfectly that the **day of the Lord** so cometh AS A THIEF in the night.

3 For when they shall say, Peace and safety; then sudden destruction cometh upon them, as travail upon a woman with child; and they shall not escape.

4 But ye, brethren, are not in darkness, that that day should overtake you as a thief.

5 Ye are all the children of light, and the children of the day: we are not of the night, nor of darkness.

6 Therefore let us not sleep, as do others; but let us watch and be sober.

7 For they that sleep sleep in the night; and they that be drunken are drunken in the night.

8 But let us, who are of the day, be sober, putting on the breastplate of faith and love; and for an helmet, the hope of salvation.

9 For God hath not appointed us to wrath, but to obtain salvation by our Lord Jesus Christ...

Paul said in verse one above that they need not ask about the timing of the rapture which he had taught them while there in Thessaly. The times and seasons are in God's hands. Before Jesus' ascension, His disciples asked Him the same question they had asked Him before He went to the cross – when Lord? When will you restore the Kingdom?

In both instances, it was a question about timing. Jesus answered them on Mt. Olive that only the Father knew the day and the hour, not man, not angels, not even the Son of Man. Because the day was an unknown factor to everyone but the Father, **he had to be referring to the rapture.**

The abomination of desolation at mid-point in the Tribulation is a known factor. Moreover, the manifestation of the Kingdom is known to come precisely 1335 days after the setting up of the abomination [Daniel 12:12]. Therefore, once the Day of the Lord begins – that's the quest of this book...when does it begin? – the entire week of seven years has numerous clearly marked events that happen precisely on time.

Because many scheduled events of the Tribulation are prophesied throughout the Old Testament and in the book of

Revelation, they do not happen as a thief coming by surprise. Paul must have meant, therefore, that the timing of the rapture of prepared believers is the unknown factor that no one can pinpoint on a calendar. Moreover, Old Testament prophets knew nothing about a Messianic church distinguished from Judaic synagogues, much less a rapture associated with it. Nevertheless, there are veiled references to it some of which I will enumerate in Chapter 5.

Jewish Customs Reveal Secrets

Knowing about Jewish customs or rituals will help in understanding that Paul was referring to rapture in both Thessalonian letters. Since rapture is associated with the 'Feast of Trumpets' and one of the names of that feast day is the 'Day of Hiding', let's see how this name denotes a rapture.

If something is hidden, it is out of sight and hence unknown. Therefore, this feast is also called the 'Day of the Awakening Blast'[3] which sound symbolizes waking up people who are sleeping so that they won't miss being raptured. Other significant names for the 'Feast of Trumpets' are the 'Coronation of the King' and 'Marriage of the Lamb' both of which hint about a rapture/wedding day.

Furthermore, 'Feast of Trumpets' is called 'Judgment Day' because Jews believe that when the set time on the calendar arrives, God judges who will not experience His wrath on sin and who will be raptured to heaven as part of the Bridehood of Jesus. It is a time of decision. God responds according to how people decide to act. Can you see how all the titles or nomenclatures for the 'Feast of Trumpets' disclose God's will for this feast day?

---

[3] The 'Feast of Trumpets' has as many as 10 names associated with it.

What is the meaning behind it being a hidden day? Trumpets are not blown on the last day of Elul immediately preceding the next day which is the 'Feast of Trumpets'. Why not? Enlightened Jews believe the trumpet-blasts on this 'Day of Hiding' are not blown so that satan would not be awakened with a sound [Psalms 89:15] and thus would not be aware that something significant is about to happen.

The symbolism connotes that the devil wants to know the day when Jesus comes to take rulership of earth away from him. For if he knows the day the Avenger of Blood aka Jesus is to arrive, he would counter-maneuver God's strategy and seduce Jesus' Bride from being rapture-ready. He almost wiped out the entire human race in Noah's day by beguiling people to doubt there would be a flood [Genesis 6:1ff]. Thank God, eight people were not seduced and made it into Noah's ark.

The Feasts of Jehovah

When God made a nation out of the Hebrews at their exodus from Egyptian slavery, He gave them a new calendar, a Sacred Calendar that starts on the spring equinox. Their long-standing creation calendar called their civil calendar begins in the fall six months later. The Lord established the Sacred Calendar for the purpose of publishing to the world His plan for redeeming humankind from the power of satan.

Leviticus chapter 23 details 7 moeds (Hebrew for 'set appointments') on specific days when God's Redeemer would accomplish redemption for humanity. The Redeemer would come to earth on these set appointments and fulfill God's will in the progressive process of wresting rulership of the world from the clutches of satan who stole it from Adam. It takes several millennia to fulfill the plan.

These feasts of Jehovah portray through rituals what each one represents related to redemption. The first four feasts were accomplished two thousand years ago in the spring exactly on the 'set times' of the calendar when Jesus Christ made His First Advent to earth. Logically, the last three feasts should be fulfilled on the 'set times' in like manner when Jesus makes His Second Advent to earth. The dictionary definition of Advent is 'a coming into being or use'.

Because the Internet is full of information regarding the Feasts of Jehovah, I will only give you their names:

1. Feast of Passover
2. Feast of Unleavened Bread
3. Feast of Firstfruits
4. Feast of Pentecost
5. Feast of Trumpets
6. Feast of Atonement
7. Feast of Tabernacles.

Is The Devil In The Details – Or Is Truth?

Since the Internet provides a lot of information about the feasts of Jehovah, I will only speak to the 'Feast of Trumpets' in brief given that it suggests a rapture. Jews associate this feast with a wedding. And because it is relevant to the premise of a Pretribulational rapture, one needs to understand its significance in God's redemption plan. As has been noted, it has many names which is probably due to the fact that it has only one ritual – the blowing of trumpets. But the primary name for Jews is 'Rosh Hashanah' meaning 'first (or head) of the year'. It is celebrated in Israel as the new year of their civil calendar, which is the 1st day of their seventh month Tishrei. It is also acclaimed to be 'the birthday of the creation of mankind'.

Sandwiched between Trumpets on the 1ˢᵗ of Tishrei and Atonement on the 10ᵗʰ of Tishrei are 'Days of Awe' that represent the Tribulational period of seven years. These days are not celebrated because they represent God's wrath and anger over sin.[4]

In orthodox Jewry, Hebrews have rituals accompanying the festivity of the feasts which typifiy the reality about which the feast connotes. For example, it is customary to blow a trumpet blast every day during the 6ᵗʰ Jewish month of Elul preceding Tishri 1, the 'Feast of Trumpets'. The blast warns people 'Judgment Day' is coming. and they had better get ready for it through repentance of sins.

As I said before, 'Judgment Day' is the day God decides who has repented fully during the 30 days of Elul and who is thus qualified to be hidden in heaven during the ten 'Days of Awe' when God vents His wrath on sin. Having missed the rapture, whoever does not repent during this second ten-day grace period, will be shut out of Heaven because on the 'Day of Atonement' ten days from the 'Feast of Trumpets', heaven's doors are shut. People who opposed God's commandment calling for repentance will be eternally lost on that day.

For emphasis, let me repeat the reason the shofar is not blown on the last day of Elul since it is relevant to why the rapture ought to occur on the 'Feast of Trumpets' in some year. The people of God do not want satan alerted to the fact that the next day is when righteous believers are taken to heaven. The

---

[4] The first and second day of every month are considered as one day by Israel because it starts with the sighting of the new moon and had to be confirmed by two people in olden times. Sometimes the sighting was too close to sundown to be observed. So they made sure the month had come by celebrating the 'New Moon' feast/festivities every month on two days. Adding those two days to the 10ᵗʰ 'Day of Atonement' makes 3 days accounted for between the 1ˢᵗ and 10ᵗʰ of Tishrei; this leaves 7 days for the 'Days of Awe' which represents the 7-year Tribulational period. God is extremely accurate with His math and 'set times' for events.

reader will have to decide for himself or herself whether these righteous believers are Church Age saints or Jewish Age saints. Or could the illusion have a double meaning as some Biblical truths do?

Whoever they are, they do not want to give satan time for possible entrapment of them. Therefore, the 'Day of Hiding' signals the start of the ten-day period called the 'Days of <u>Awe</u>' – an <u>awe</u>somely horrendous time for people who do not make it into heaven on 'Judgment Day'. (Doesn't this sound like rapture?). During these 'Days of Awe', while righteous people are hiding in heaven, God revenges Himself against sinners on earth. Scripture teaches that *worthy* people who escape the Tribulation by rapture will be in hiding in heaven as noted below…

Zephaniah 2:3

3 Seek ye the Lord, all ye meek of the earth, which have wrought his judgment; seek righteousness (*salvation through Jesus*), seek meekness (*teachability about rapture*): it may be **ye shall be <u>hid</u> in the day** of the Lord's anger.

Who does Zephaniah say will be hidden? The righteous meek who have repented, accepted Jesus as God the Savior, and made themselves ready for ***escape*** to heaven.

Since Jesus knew about the symbolic rituals of Jewry, His remark that no one knows the day or the hour of His return [Matthew 24:36] must have been a veiled reference to another name Hebrews have for the 'Feast of Trumpets': 'The Day No One Knows The Day Or The Hour'. The symbolism in this title and the title 'Day of Hiding' is to emphasize its unknown sudden arrival in like manner that a thief arrives in the dark to cover his covert coming.

In truth, no one does know the year Jesus will appear to rapture His Bride from earth's coming devastation even though He gave His disciples signs about the season. Considering the planet's escalating and intensifying natural and manmade (think covid-19) disasters, we are in the season. Even satan knows his time is short.

Are you Rapture-Ready?

CHAPTER -4

COMFORT AND ENCOURAGEMENT

In Chapter 3 of this essay, we examined First Thessalonians 5:1-9 where Paul explains to the troubled new converts in Thessalonica that they would not go through the terrible wrath associated with the Day of the Lord. It is without a doubt a day of woe for all people on the planet since it is God's judgmental Day of Vengeance against sin for all nations.

Interpreting the Bible literally and taking the meaning of the words at face value, the Scripture passages in both Thessaly letters clearly teach that the body of Christ will not experience any part of the Day of Vengeance. The pronouns are evidence signifying that rapture precedes Tribulation.

1 Thessalonians 5:1-9

5:1 But of the times and the seasons, brethren, **ye** have no need that I write unto **you**.

2 For **your**selves know perfectly that the day of the Lord so cometh as a thief in the night.

3 For when **they** shall say, Peace and safety; then sudden destruction cometh upon **them**, as travail upon a woman with child; and **they** shall not escape.

4 But **ye**, brethren, are not in darkness, that that day should overtake **you** as a thief.

5 **Ye** are all the children of light, and the children of the day: **we** are not of the night, nor of darkness.

6 Therefore let **us** not sleep, as do others; but let **us** watch and be sober.

7 For **they** that sleep sleep in the night; and **they** that be drunken are drunken in the night.

8 But let **us**, who are of the day, be sober, putting on the breastplate of faith and love; and for an helmet, the hope of salvation.

9 For God hath not appointed **us** to wrath, but to obtain salvation by our Lord Jesus Christ,

The entire tenor of the passage above plainly shows that Paul was writing to give believers in Thessalonica comfort and encouragement to quit fearing that they had entered the Day of the Lord. Paul exhorts them to recall what he had taught them the three weeks he was in Thessalonica during which time he explained what Jesus said about believers being snatched off earth before the Tribulation period begins [1 Thessalonians 4:15].

Assimilating chapter four of First Thessalonians with chapter five reveals that the believers ...*__knew perfectly__ that the day of the Lord so cometh as a thief in the night*. Because these believers regularly attended the synagogue and were familiar with Old Testament Scriptures, they were knowledgeable about the Day of the Lord. It was not a mystery to be revealed to them.

Rapture, however, was a mystery doctrine concealed in the scrolls of the Old Testament [Colossians 1:25-27]. Yet a few Old Testament prophets alluded to it as did the patriarchs in their Testaments written for their heritage. Paul often wrote, *I would not have you ignorant brethren concerning matters* relating to the change of dispensations [Romans 1:13; 11:25; 1

Corinthians 10:1; 12:1; 1 Thessalonians 4:13], and rapture was one of those matters.

Considering that the Day of the Lord is predominantly one of woe, wrath, darkness, and judgment as Chapter 3 documents, let us now consider what the Day of Christ infers. It contrasts with the Day of the Lord, and Paul mentions it in numerous places in his letters as a day of blessing [1 Corinthians 1:7, 8; 5:5; 2 Corinthians 1:14; Philippians 1:6; etc.].

The Day of Christ vis-à-vis The Day of the Lord

The Day of Christ is God's 'set time' that believers start living with Christ forever in heaven. It terminates the Church Age by rapturing Jesus' body off earth; whereas, the Day of the Lord begins the final millennia of human history before God creates a new heaven and earth. But, before setting up the final Messianic Age, God judges wickedness and cleanses the earth.

The Messianic Kingdom starts with Tribulation as described in the book of Revelation, and it ends after the Millennial reign of Christ. The two prophetic days of note are close in proximity, perhaps the same day, but their function differs because the Day of Christ closes the Age of Grace and the Day of the Lord restores the Age of Israel for her last week of Israel's determined time [Daniel 9:24-27]. In that respect, their function differs although they might happen on the same day. Together they could be considered a 'Day of Destiny' for the world. I'll come back to that.

The underlined and emboldened pronouns support a presumption that there are two distinctly different groups of people in this passage. One group is of the day and they miss the Tribulation; the second group is of darkness and enter the

Day of the Lord. By contrasting the second person pronouns 'ye', 'you', 'us', and 'we' with those of the third person pronouns 'they' and 'them', one can easily divide the people into two groups – children of light and children of night.

True believers are not in darkness; and therefore should not be sleeping. They should be alert looking for Christ's return as Paul writes in Titus 2:13: *Looking for that blessed hope, and the glorious appearing of the great God and our Savior Jesus Christ.* According to Paul, Jesus is coming for believers looking for him. [See Hebrews 9:28 confirming this fact.] So, children of the day ought to be watching with eager anticipation for the Lord to snatch us off this wicked planet and take us to our glorious home in heaven.

Paul ends his encouraging letter to Thessaly with the admonition that believers stand fast and secure themselves with the powerful forces of faith, hope, and love [verse 8]. But, the most encouraging of all his statements is that believers *are not appointed to wrath, but to obtain salvation* (deliverance from wrath) *by our Lord Jesus Christ* [verse 9]. Surely, this ought to give us reason to comfort one another.

If language means anything, this passage in First Thessalonians distinguishes between people who are rapture-ready and those who will engage Tribulation. Children of the night have not put on the helmet of salvation and hence have no hope of deliverance. They are the ones who are appointed unto wrath. The only reason they are appointed to wrath is because they will have rejected the gift of salvation afforded people through Jesus' work of the cross [1 John 2:2]. In essence, they <u>have appointed themselves</u> to wrath by refusing God's gracious <u>gift</u> of Jesus' substitutionary payment for their sin debt [2 Kings 17:17].

In rejecting so great salvation, unbelievers' choices will cause them great suffering. It is bewildering that so many people who know they will die one day are more interested in the pleasures of this world and selfish ambitions than in securing their eternal welfare. Amazingly, most people are unaware that they are only one breath away from eternity.

The word 'comfort' is used four times in First Thessalonians and once in Paul's second letter to them. Obviously then, Paul wrote these letters to comfort people who read them. Note that verse 11 ends the passage in chapter 5 saying: *Wherefore, comfort yourselves together and edify one another even as also ye do.*

The word 'wherefore' is an adverb referring to all the verses preceding it that exhort people not to fear. In them, Paul explained the difference between children of darkness who enter the Day of the Lord and children of light who experience the Day of Christ. So we can say that the word 'wherefore' supports the reason we are to comfort each other.

I submit there is unmistakably no comfort in knowing one has to endure the wrath of Almighty God on sin in the day of judgment. His wrath fell on sin once before at the flood, and the world was totally devastated. Therefore, comfort is in knowing that rapture precedes the awful day of God's wrath on sin, the next time by fire.

Summary of 1 Thessalonians

Our Lord gave the mystery revelation about rapture in Paul's letters to Thessaly, and it has been preserved in the New Testament canon and passed down through the church. Resurrection of dead believers and translation of living believers at rapture applies only to persons who are 'in Christ', to whomsoever has made Jesus Lord and Savior and is walking in the light of life.

The first letter to Thessaly explains that believers in Christ ought not be concerned that they will enter the Tribulation because they are children of light and are not appointed to the Tribulational wrath of God. The personal pronouns underscore that believers escape the Tribulation; therefore, the letter was written to comfort and encourage believers that they do not have to brace for scourging as naysayers of a Pretrib rapture purport.

Paul's Second Letter to the Thessalonians

Now let's look at Paul's second letter to the Thessalonians in which he further documents that believers will not experience Tribulation.

2 Thessalonians 2:1-8
1 Now we beseech you, brethren, by the coming of our Lord Jesus Christ, and by our gathering together unto him,

2 That ye be not soon shaken in mind, or be troubled, neither by spirit, nor by word, nor by letter as from us, as that <u>the DAY OF CHRIST</u> is at hand.

3 Let no man deceive you by any means: for **that day** shall not come, except there come a falling away first, and that **man of sin** be revealed, **the son of perdition**;

4 Who opposeth and exalteth himself above all that is called God, or that is worshipped; so that he as God sitteth in the temple of God, shewing himself that he is God.

5 Remember ye not, that, when I was yet with you, I told you these things?

6 And now ye know what withholdeth (*restrains*) that he might be revealed in his time.

7 For the mystery of iniquity doth already work: only he who now letteth (*prevents or restrains*) will let (*prevent or restrain*), until he be taken out of the way.

8 And then shall that Wicked (*one*) be revealed, whom the Lord shall consume with the spirit of his mouth, and shall destroy with the brightness of his coming:

Fear Causes Confusion

From the opening verses of chapter two above, we learn that believers in Thessaly were disturbed and frightened because they had received false information contradicting what Paul had taught them while he was with them. They were intelligent people but they were new converts to the Grace Age and unschooled in the mystery revelation given to Paul about rapture on the Day of Christ [verse 2].

Paul reminded them he had taught them these things when he was there [verse 5]. And since he was there only three weeks, he considered it a foundational doctrine to the gospel of Christ. But, after writing his first letter, false teachers confused and induced the Thessalonians to believe that they had missed the rapture and that the Day of the Lord was upon them due to increased persecution by governmental powers.

Is Falling Away A Departure?

The passage of Scripture above is talking about governmental changes that will occur when Christ comes to snatch His Bride away from Tribulation. Those changes are noted in verse 2 as the Day of Christ. Both the Day of the Lord and the Day of Christ although technically not the same will usher in significant changes in how society is governed. With a lot of people disappearing all over the world at rapture, economies will be disrupted and governments will seek for a leader who can bring order out of chaos. Reread the above passage so you have a clear picture of how Paul explained the progression of events that closes the Grace Age and ushers in the Kingdom Age.

Being a 'Day of Destiny' for all people, it behooves one to understand that the words 'that day' in verse 3 are referring to one significant day regardless of its name. Paul said in his second letter to Thessaly: *Let no man deceive you by any means for <u>that day</u> shall not come except there come a <u>falling away</u> FIRST* [verse 3 above]. The day noted as 'that day' was the Day of Christ aka rapture, an irrevocable day be it the Day of Christ or the Day of the Lord. Both days point to different dispensational administrations by God.

The word 'first' in the Greek does not mean simply 'prior to', but the more common usage is 'foremost in time, place, order, or importance'. Hence, it means 'FIRST OF ALL'. So, the *falling away* precedes a day of great change in God's ordered management of earth. It is truly a 'Day of Destiny'.

The Greek word for 'falling away' is *apostasia* and this Greek word means a 'defection', 'forsaking', or 'departure'. Most Bible scholars take this to mean a forsaking of the true doctrines of Christ leading to a lukewarm church, the Laodicean problem of Revelation chapter three. The forsaking of truth is happening in the church today indicating that the Laodicean era has arrived. But there always have been people who defect from truth after accepting Jesus as the only means of Eternal Life, even during Apostle Paul's pilgrimage on earth.

Departure from sound doctrine is not easily observed by Christians pocketed in the world in nations that are not primarily Christian. However, in the United States of America, it is quite visible. Most of the professors and instructors in seminaries and Bible schools today are similar to the Pharisees of Jesus' time and have rejected many of the apostolic doctrines of the early church as they follow the teaching or traditions of men. This is secular humanism at work.

Wise men by human standards have forgotten, if they ever knew, that the Bible says the wisdom of this world is foolishness with God and the weakness of God is stronger than man [1 Corinthians 1:25]. Because of worldly arrogance, it pleased God to choose the foolishness of preaching a cross to save people by faith alone in a crucified man and not intellectual knowledge or human wisdom [1 Corinthians 2:1-5]. God has confounded the wise, the strong, and the rich with the simplicity of faith so that no flesh glories in His presence [Jeremiah 9:23, 24].

Gnostic Heresy

When Paul wrote his letters to the Thessalonians, there was spreading abroad a teaching that Jesus did not physically rise from death but rather rose up in spirit only. Thus, they say He does not have a resurrected physical body. This concept is a Gnostic teaching that began in the first century and still lives today under different labels.

It takes a physical body to contact physical matter and control physical things. Since satan is a spirit without a physical body, he sells this lie concerning Jesus to delude people who do not know Scripture. The devil needs a body to contact earthly things which is why demons seek embodiment of people. Even pigs will do as earth-suits as we learn from Jesus when He healed the demoniac at Gadara [Mark 5:1-20]. When people believe a lie, they have in effect sold themselves to the devil's rule as Adam and Eve did in the garden.

Apostle John's epistles were written especially to refute the Gnostic heresy that Jesus did not rise up bodily with a glorified body. Regrettably, this Gnostic lie is gaining ground among churchgoers today, but it is way too vast a subject to try to cover here. Some books of the New Testament direct attention to correcting issues related to it such as Colossians and the epistle of First John. Gnosticism tickles and excites man's intellect at the expense of the simplicity of the gospel of Jesus; and it is satanically inspired to subvert the souls of men to perdition.

An Alternative Concept of Departure

In contrast to the Greek language meaning of *apostasia* as a 'falling away' from truth, which is what most Biblicists teach today, let me offer an alternative interpretation for this word which is explained below and is equally valid and acceptable in Greek parlance. I am not implying the interpretation of 'falling away' from truth is wrong. Rather I want to submit that both interpretations are applicable to this verse in the same way that the titles Son of Man and Son of God are both applicable to Jesus.

Because the Biblical law of double reference is a valid hermeneutical principle, both titles apply to Jesus thereby revealing Jesus' unique 'hypostatic union' of a spiritual person, Son of God, and a physical one, Son of Man. Double meanings are common in Scripture.

The alternative meaning of *apostasia* is 'a departure'. Many Ante-Nicene church fathers subscribed to this definition. People such as William Tyndale along with most forerunners to the translation of the 1611 King James Bible used the word 'departure' instead of 'falling away' in their translations. Moreover, more than a few notable contemporary scholars hold to it as a valid interpretation of this verse.

If we use 'departure' as the intended meaning of *apostasia,* Apostle Paul was referring to the fact that the true church of born-again believers **must depart** earth in rapture prior to the appearance of the Day of the Lord and the man of sin. This is in keeping with Paul's teaching in both his letters to Thessaly.

In Paul's second letter, he beseeches believers to remember what he had taught them while with them about *the coming of our Lord Jesus Christ and our gathering together unto him in the air* (Day of Christ) so as not to get anxious that Tribulation had arrived [verses 1 and 2 above]. In my opinion, the words '*by our gathering together unto him in the air*' unlock the meaning of *apostasia* as 'departing from earth' although it could mean 'departure from truth'.

Can you see that Paul is appealing to what the Thessalonians knew about the rapture? He continues in his second letter to admonish them not to be shaken in mind or be troubled by false teaching that the Day of Tribulation had arrived. He implored them not to accept the fake report that they had missed the rapture on grounds that it could not have come since they were still alive on earth and the man of sin had not come forth in the Temple declaring himself to be god. If he had, the whole empire would know about it.

It is obvious from this passage Paul wanted rapture-hopefuls to understand that because they had not *departed* earth, the rapture had not occurred, and therefore, the Day of Christ could not have come. That is the meaning of *apostasia* to which I subscribe.

When Does the Man of Sin Appear?

In 2 Thessalonians 2:3, two of the 30 or so titles that refer to the Antichrist appear – *man of sin* and *son of perdition*. As the last gentile ruler of earth, he finalizes Adam's earth lease. I suggest that the parable in Mark 12:1-11 is an allusion to Adam's lease of earth.

As reported previously, God scheduled the earth lease to run for 6,000 years, the time period inferred in Genesis 2:4 where it is recorded that the generations of earth numbered similarly as the days of the creation of earth. The correlation of 6,000 years with 6 days is mentioned in 2 Peter 3:8: *But, beloved, be not ignorant of this one thing, that one day is with the Lord as a thousand years, and a thousand years as one day.*

The Kinsman-Redeemer: God's Second Adam

God knew before the creation that man would sin. So God planned for a Kinsman-Redeemer, the anointed Messiah, to come rescue the creation from certain death and destruction. The Kinsman-Redeemer who would liberate earth from satan's control was a second Adam having the same creative configuration or like genome of the first Adam. We know Him as God's Son, the One appointed heir of all things [Hebrews 1:2] due to His having paid the ransom price for redeeming God's creation from the curse.[Mark 10:45].

Only two humans were created directly by God. Both were called Adam and both were called sons of God [Luke 3:38]. Due to sin, all progeny of the first Adam are born with his sin nature. The Bible says that the life of the flesh is in the blood [Leviticus 17:11], and the blood of all human babies comes from the father's genes. Since Jesus was born of a virgin without a human father, He was exempted from Adam's sin nature. Can you see why a virgin birth was imperative?

Because the blood comes from the father, it was necessary that God supply the complimentary 23 chromosomes to Mary's so as to be born with human DNA. Hence, Jesus was a direct creation of God – a second Adam and truly a Son of God [Luke 1:23]. Having the genes of Mary, He was truly human and had the possibility of sinning as Adam did. Since He was born without a sin nature and having lived a sinless life, He died a wrongful death because it is sin that condemns men to die [Romans 6:23].

Thankfully, the second Adam Jesus lived a perfect sinless life qualifying Him to pay the sin price of death for man's redemption. Had He sinned, He would have needed a Savior Himself. This second Son of God is called 'the Christ' (Greek) or 'the Messiah' (Hebrew) meaning 'The Anointed One' of God. He is 'The Anointed One' because He is the One appointed and empowered by God to recover His creation. Anointing means empowerment.

Contradistinctively, Paul calls the 'man of sin' the 'son of perdition' because he will become the embodiment of his father the devil [John 8:44] who will indwell and empower the Antichrist as the Holy Spirit indwells and empowers believers. Therefore, the *man of sin* is called Anti-Christ (Anti means against) due to his being 'the anointed one' of satan who opposes Christ, 'The Anointed Jesus'. He will exalt himself as God and demand worship. People who refuse will be beheaded.

Revelation 20:4
4 And I saw thrones, and they sat upon them, and judgment was given unto them: and I saw the souls of them that were <u>beheaded</u> for the witness of Jesus, and for the word of God, and which had not worshipped the beast, neither his image, neither had received his mark upon their foreheads, or in their hands; and they lived and reigned with Christ a thousand years.

Antichrist Overcomes Saints in the Tribulation

Scripture reports that Antichrist will overcome the saints of God in Daniel 7:21 and 8:24 as well as in the book of Revelation: *It was given unto him* (the Antichrist) *to make war with the saints, and to overcome them* [Revelation 13:7]. Remember that the true church is not on earth during this time; so, Jesus' prophecy that the gates of hell shall not prevail against His church will prove correct [Matthew 16:18]. During the Tribulation, the church is gone and no longer accepting applicants because the Grace Age will have been closed at the rapture of the Bride.

Saints who are overcome by the Antichrist will be people who accepted Jesus as their Savior during the Tribulation era; and there will be many because their eyes will be opened when they see the true church gone. Enoch, the seventh from Adam, wrote in his book eons ago that the rapture's purpose at the end of days is to warn earth-dwellers who missed it to repent. By carelessly sleeping through the myriad of cosmic and terrestrial signals that the wrath of God was approaching they forfeit escape from God's wrath.

Enoch's prophecy corroborates Apocalyptic prophecy indicating there will be a countless number of martyrs beheaded by Antichrist [Revelation 6:9-11 with 20:4]. The martyred saints, unfortunately, will not be a part of the Bride of Christ even though they make it into heaven at their death because they were not rapture-ready when the trumpet sounded [Matthew 25:12]. They will die because the wicked man of sin will have come on the scene plying his reign of terror.

When Does the Man of Sin Manifest?

Paul explained the order of events that trigger the Tribulation in 2 Thessalonians 2:6-8. In those verses, he says that something holds back or restrains the Antichrist from making an appearance. In verse 5, he reminds them that he had told them before of these things.

2 Thessalonians 2:5-8

5 Remember ye not, that, when I was yet with you, I told you these things?

6 And now ye know what withholdeth (*restrains*) that he might be revealed in his time.

7 For the mystery of iniquity doth already work: only he who now letteth (*hinders or restrains*) will let (*hinder or restrain*), until he be taken out of the way.

8 And <u>THEN</u> shall that Wicked (*one*) be revealed, whom the Lord shall consume with the spirit of his mouth, and shall destroy with the brightness of his coming:

According to verse 8 above, the man of sin appears immediately after Jesus' Bride vanishes. The something that withholds iniquity mentioned in verse 6 is the church indwelt by the Holy Spirit. Without Holy Spirit empowerment, the church would be no match for the devil and his cohorts. Hence, when the church raptures, the restrainer of evil will have been removed. The Bride will have eloped safely with Jesus to her wedding in heaven.

We know from verse four of chapter 2 in Paul's second letter that this wicked man opposes all that is called God. He even sits in the temple of God showing himself that he is God. The reason he is able to overcome church saints left behind and rule as a demigod over the whole world is because the force that has been holding wickedness in check will be gone. What is that something hindering iniquity from running rampant over the whole earth? What keeps sin, evil, and lawlessness under wraps so that it cannot manifest its final full fury?

1 John 4:4
4 Ye are of God, little children, and have overcome them: because greater is he (*the Holy Spirit)* that is in you, than he that is in the world.

We know from the above Scripture that the greater one in regenerated Christians is the Holy Spirit who was sent by the Father and Son to empower members of His family. Being God, nothing can overpower God. This truth alone is why believers are masters of evil spirits. If Christians realized that the might of the universe lives inside them, the world would not be on the verge of self-destructing. But alas, church leaders have been remiss for the most part in teaching Christians who they are 'in Christ' and what belongs to them by virtue of being 'in Christ'.

Apostle John talks about antichrist spirits in his three letters to the church. And in chapter 2:20 and 27 of First John, Apostle John reveals that Christians are anointed because the Holy Spirit lives inside them, and they need not be deceived by the evil one ruling the cosmos.

Because the Holy Spirit indwells believers, His empowerment is such that antichrist spirits cannot overcome us believers – unless we let them as verse 1 of chapter 4 intimates. This establishes the truth that the Holy Spirit dwelling in born-again believers is the restraining force hindering final expression of the antichrist spirit. When righteous saints depart in rapture, the restraint on sin vanishes as Isaiah confirms.

Isaiah 57:1
1 The righteous perisheth (*vanishes*), and no man layeth it to heart: and merciful men are taken away, none considering that the righteous is taken away (*through rapture*) from the evil to come.

Summary of 2 Thessalonians

We have established from Scripture when the man of sin appears. It will be after the rapture of the true church. The lid on iniquity is the Holy Spirit working through born-again believers because He is the only One with power enough to restrict people from doing all the wicked things they are bent on doing. So when will the restraint be removed? When the church raptures, Antichrist's restraint is removed.

Rapture of the true church does not mean the Holy Spirit will be absent from the Tribulation period. He is God, and God is omnipresent. He will be convicting people of sin even during the Tribulation just as He did throughout the Old Testament era when he did not indwell people.

The Holy Spirit's Presence within believers has empowered them to testify for Jesus and do His works, a gifting that has held iniquity in check. When that empowerment is gone, evil will escalate at a rapid pace because humanity's preservative salt, the church, will have been taken 'out of the midst of' the earth. Born-again believers keep earth from putrefying; but, when the salt is gone, decay comes swiftly. (Ante-Nicene fathers believed that 'out of the midst of' was Hebraic code for the church's rapture out of Tribulation.)

To further emphasize that it is the Holy Spirit <u>within</u> the body of Christ that is holding back sin, let me remind you that it is the Holy Spirit's assignment in the Church Age to find, prepare, and deliver a Bride to Christ. We have been given a beautiful picture of this in the Old Testament's account of Abraham sending his servant to find a bride for Isaac, the son that he loved so dearly. This picture is a prophetic type of the real thing that has to come to pass in the last days (the antitype).

A Bride for the Son

Abraham sent his servant to find a bride for Isaac in a far country. Similarly, God the Father sent the Holy Spirit from the throne room to earth [John 15:26] to select a Bride for His Son Jesus. The servant found a willing bride for Isaac, Rebecca, in a faraway country, and the Holy Spirit has been finding among gentiles countless persons who want to become betrothed to Jesus as their Lord. Like Rebecca, the majority of these people live far away from the Son's heavenly homeland called New Jerusalem [Revelation 21:2]. Gifts were given to Rebecca prior to her betrothal, and the Holy Spirit has been giving spiritual gifts to the body of Christ since the church's inception in antitypical fashion. Reception of the gifts by a woman signifies a betrothal commitment on the part of the bride. She is considered wedded even though the marriage is not consummated.

Having received expensive gifts as tokens of her prospective husbands worth and commitment to being an honorable provider of a spouse, Rebecca made the journey to her new distant home without having seen her husband-to-be with great anticipation of a perfect marriage. Her expectant eager husband Isaac left his tent in the family compound to come out into the desert to meet his beautiful bride. In like manner, Jesus will descend from heaven to mountain-top level to meet His Bride in the air.

The Bride of the church awaits One *whom having not seen, ye love; in whom though now ye see him not, yet believing, ye rejoice with joy unspeakable and full of glory* [1 Peter 1:9]. True believers are ecstatic at the thought of journeying to their new heavenly home in rapture when Jesus comes down from heaven with a shout and trumpet blast to call up His Bride 'in clouds'. Both Rebecca and the church return to their father's house for the wedding. How much more alike could a type and its antitype be?

We now know when the Antichrist appears. After the restrainer is *taken out of the way, <u>THEN</u> shall that wicked (one) be revealed.* The adverbial word of time 'then' pins it down. When the Holy Spirit delivers the Bride to the Bridegroom, the restrainer is gone and the planet will return to the days of the Age of Israel because the dispensation of Grace will be over. With the salt gone, things go downhill fast.

The Conclusion of Confusion is Delusion

2 Thessalonians 2:9-12
9 Even him [*the Antichrist*], whose coming is after the working of Satan with all power and signs and <u>lying wonders</u>, [*confusion abounds*]
10 And with all deceivableness of unrighteousness in them that perish; because they received not the love of the truth, that they might be saved.

11 And for this cause God shall send them <u>strong delusion</u>, that they should believe a lie:

12 That they all might be <u>damned</u> (*conclusion*) who believed not the truth, but had pleasure in unrighteousness.

Having no restraint, satan will work diligently *with all deceivableness of unrighteousness* to seduce the world into worshipping him. The Bible prophesies he will use great signs and lying wonders with which to deceive people. Furthermore, Scripture indicates that earth-dwellers who refuse God's offer of escape through Jesus and rapture will succumb to strong delusion and be eternally damned. This dangerous foreboding [2:9-12 above] happens because people *believed not the truth* about a rapture freeing one from the Tribulational woes *but had pleasure in unrighteousness.*

Are you Rapture-Ready?

CHAPTER -5

THE RAPTURE IN THE OLD TESTAMENT

As noted in the previous chapter, anyone missing the rapture will risk losing his head by the guillotine if he or she chooses not to worship the Antichrist during his rule of earth [Revelation 20:4]. Times will be tough and persons who do not join in with the ecumenical movement that merges all faiths into a one-world religion will be sought out and exterminated.

Preaching Jesus as the exclusive and only way to the heavenly Father [John 14:6] will be dangerous, disallowed, and immediately squashed by totalitarian governmental watchdogs. Tribulational woes as depicted in John's book of Revelation are not imaginative incidents to a make-believe or fake novel. Rather, what I have been describing in this treatise is scripted in the Bible through prophecy. And if God said it, it will surely come to pass. Are you rapture-ready?

The Philadelphian Mandate

Before the rapture occurs, we have a window of opportunity to reach as many people as possible with the gospel of Christ because Jesus is holding open the door for

Philadelphians to get the Word of Jesus Christ to the four corners of the world.

Revelation 3:8

8 I know thy works: behold, I have set before thee an open door, and no man can shut it: for thou hast a little strength, and hast kept my word, and hast not denied my name.

The true church of born-again believers does not mix truth with secular strategies promoting globalist ideals and social reforms. Therefore, Jesus holds open the door for His salvation message to go forth into the entire world for an endtime harvest of souls beyond anything we can imagine. Satan's evil coved-19 pandemic has softened the ground for revival which is the reason God permitted it. Behind current events, God works all things to fulfill His will and prophecy.

A great awakening concerning eternal matters has begun, and it will continue into the Tribulation after rapture. When harvest time is over and the body of Christ is complete, the door of opportunity to miss the hour of temptation will be shut as the true Philadelphian church is seized off earth before its judgment by God. The Church Age will have ended, and lukewarm Laodiceans who combine truth with worldly ideals will enter the Tribulation.

According to Old Testament patriarch Enoch in his book, there will be an enormous harvest of the souls finding Eternal Life [Revelation 7:9, 14] after rapturites vanish from earth. But sadly, Laodiceans will realize too late that they had not purified themselves to make the rapture and thus will join Tribulation's martyred people. Total separation from worldliness is required for the Bridehood because Apostle James warns us that friendship with the world is enmity with God [James 4:4].

Some earth-dwellers will at once repent when Tribulation starts and make white their robes [Revelation 7:13, 14] so that they are not disgraced and wind up in hell; but others will not. We deceive ourselves if we think we will be raptured while continuing to live in sin. Jesus admonishes us to ...*hold fast that which thou hast, that no man take thy crown* [Revelation 3:11]. In other words, it is possible that false doctrines promoted by false teachers can snatch away our kingship privilege. So we must be careful to hold fast to sound doctrine through Bible study, to stay alert and rapture-ready for our Lord's return.

Old Testament prophets spoke of the day of God's vengeance at least twenty-seven times in the Scriptures warning that in flaming fire and anger God will take vengeance on persons who reject His glorious salvation through His Son Jesus [2 Thessalonians 1:6-8]. If believers are merely protected spectators on earth in this time of vengeance as Midtrib and Posttrib people say, then we would <u>not</u> be kept <u>from</u> the '*hour of testing*' man's allegiance to the true God,

Will a person be willing to die rather than worship satan and take his mark? The temptation to take the mark of the beast in order to stay alive is what is meant by the '*hour of temptation*'. So, the protracted 7 years of great hardship is God's longsufferingness to give people opportunity not to *be punished with everlasting destruction from the presence of the Lord* [2 Thessalonians 1:9]. No, dear one, the Bible says we are kept **from** the *hour of temptation,* the entire time of progressively severe cataclysmic events.

Over and over Jesus declares that He is coming quickly, [Revelation 3:11; 22:7, 12, 20], like a thief [3:3; 16:15], therefore, we ought to be ready. For what should we be ready? We **must** be ready for our marriage at rapture in heaven. Jesus is not telling us to get ready to be flogged with the horrors of

God's righteous indignation. A bridegroom who loves his bride comes to rescue her from danger, not sit aloof and watch as she undergoes anguish for lack of the necessities of life.

Because Jesus loves the church, as a trustworthy Bridegroom, He gave Himself for our guilt liability to death [Matthew 8:17], paid the price for our freedom, and made a way for our escape. For this reason, our Lord exhorts us to keep looking up for our redemption draws near.

Whoever believes a saved individual must go through Tribulation, then that believer is not looking for a Savior but for the Antichrist. Since Jesus comes quickly, if you aren't looking for Him, you might miss Him. Don't become preoccupied with the cares of this world because this planet is not our home [Colossians 3:1-3], and we are in the season. Our home is the New Jerusalem in heaven with our beloved Savior [Hebrews 12:22-24].

Old Testament Scriptures Concealing the Rapture Event

Some naysayers about rapture argue that it is not taught in the Old Testament; therefore, there's no prophetic evidence warranting it as a major doctrine of Christianity. Scornfully, they call Pretribulationism a secret doctrine without Scriptural validity.

Following are some Scriptures that countermand their contention it is not found in the Old Testament. Why did God conceal in the Old Testament His plans to make human beings temples of God after Jesus rose from the dead? If the devil knew what God was planning to do in resurrecting Jesus from death – putting Christ inside the body of a believer – he would not have crucified the Lord of glory and relinquished his authority of death to Jesus [1 Corinthians 2:6-8].

Colossians 1:27

27 To whom God would make known what is the riches of the glory of this mystery among the Gentiles; which is Christ in you, the hope of glory:

Because Jesus and a believer are one spirit [1 Corinthians 6:17], a truly born-again believer has everything belonging to Christ – His love, His grace, His authority, His power, His joy, His faith, His patience, etc. Especially significant is the indwelling presence of His Spirit, the power source that created the universe and raised Jesus from death [Ephesians 1:19, 20].

If satan had known that God was going to indwell believers thereby making them masters over him, he would not have used his premier weapon of death to destroy Jesus. Therefore, the glorious gospel Paul wanted all people to know about was the truth that Jesus desires to live inside people in order to confront, confound, and crush satan's dominion by giving believers the power of attorney to use Jesus' name. *For without me* (Jesus) *you can do nothing* [John 15:5].

Jesus' resurrection destroyed satan's death grip of fear [Hebrews 2:14, 15] whereby he is not able to terrify people any more unless they let him. Satan no longer has the keys of death and hell, Jesus does [Revelation 1:18], and no one has to be bound by satan if they will make Jesus their Lord instead of remaining a pawn in the dominion of darkness.

Scripture #1:

Micah 7:1-2

7:1 Woe is me! for I am as when they have gathered (*harvested and taken away*) the summer fruits, as the grape gleanings of the vintage: there is no cluster to eat: my soul desired the firstripe fruit.

2 <u>The good man is perished</u> (*vanished*) <u>out of the earth</u>: and there is none upright among men: they all lie in wait for blood; they hunt every man his brother with a net.

This passage in Micah (read the whole chapter), pictures Israel's punishment for idolatry in the near view when Micah prophesied as well as in a faraway time frame at the end of her 2,500-year-old pilgrimage of persecution. Sorry to say, Jews persistently ignore God's counsel about disobedience to His instructions. Even today she has not carefully studied the Tanakh, the Hebrew Scriptures, nor has she researched Daniel 9:24-27 where she is apprised about a dangerous treaty she ought not have confirmed with an Antichrist person in the latter days.

Micah depicts with words Israel's upcoming destruction due to her refusal to repent of disobedience in following God. The near destruction in Micah's day of Northern Israel by Assyria is a type of the faraway antitype endtime holocaust of Israel during the Tribulation when Jacob's troubling birth brings forth the Kingdom Age. This is a classic example of type and antitype.

It is reported that most Israelis today are secularists or atheists and ignore Scripture. Perhaps that's the reason they are trying to make peace with the Palestinians who want them completely uprooted and removed from their God-given land. They do not know the prophecies such as Micah's which cautions about consorting with their blood-sworn enemies who want them annihilated. Blinded by self-deception, orthodox Jewry will make a *covenant with death* when her only real friends *vanish* from earth in rapture. Being duped, they will covenant with the Antichrist in exchange for peace and security.

Isaiah 28:15, 18

15 Because ye have said, We have made a <u>covenant with death</u>, and with hell are we at agreement; when the overflowing scourge shall pass through, it shall not come unto us: for **we have made lies our refuge, and under falsehood have we hid ourselves**:…

18 And your <u>covenant with death</u> shall be disannulled, and your agreement with hell shall not stand; when the overflowing scourge shall pass through, <u>then ye shall be trodden down by it</u>.

Israel will languish during the Tribulation period because, according to the above, her enemies will trample her down. In partial fulfillment of this prophecy, she has given away much land for peace already. A lot of the land she claims was acquired by a God-orchestrated supernatural conquest in the 1967 war with her Arab neighbors.

Disregarding God's handiwork whereby Israel's borders enlarged from the spoils of war, she has heretofore stupidly offered to divide Jerusalem and to withdraw from the West Bank as she did from Gaza to her dismay. But amazingly, the Palestinians are as duped as she is because they refused the offer – not once, but twice!

Nonetheless, according to the above passages of Scripture in Micah and Isaiah, Israel will make a *covenant with death*. Making lies her refuge instead of the Word of the Lord, she will be severely terrorized and trodden down by the Antichrist [Isaiah 28:18].

Today, Israel's only real friends are born-again Christians, but they will be raptured off the planet leaving her to fend for herself. When this happens, because she is so tiny among the nations, she will not survive Tribulation's horrors. Antichrist who hates her will bring upon her a worst holocaust than she endured in WWII; for this scourging will be satan's last attempt to strike out at God and he knows it.

Micah laments Israel's situation by saying that her only friends, *the good men* – the true church – are *perished out of the earth.* 'Perished' is an English translation of the Hebrew *avad min eretz* which actually means "vanished '*out of*' the earth". Can you see that it is referring to the true church having been raptured 'out of' sight? Because they are gone, the prophet says that there is none upright among men to help Israel. World anarchy will be widespread, and every man will be a prey for predators. Hence, Israel is without friends after the rapture.

In verse one of Micah, we see in the word 'gathered' a picture of the summer crops having been harvested and nothing left to eat. 'Gathered' means 'to take away' or 'to remove'. The fruit of born-again believers will have been taken away and put into the barns in heaven. Harvest is over and nothing is left on earth but tares and weeds which will be burned up [Malachi 4:1].

Scripture #2:

Psalms 12:1
12:1 Help, Lord; for the godly man ceaseth (*to be complete*); for the faithful fail (*vanish*) from among the children of men.....

In this Psalm through verse 5a, David laments about the Tribulation's catastrophic period of history. Like Micah, the verse explains that godly men are gone. Hebrew for 'ceaseth' is *gamar* which astoundingly means 'the godly are completed'. In other words, the body of Christ <u>is complete</u> and has vanished to heaven to be with her head Jesus. See how accurate prophecy is?

The Psalmist cries for help because now the tiny nation of Israel is without friends in a wicked world. She is shocked by the disappearance of millions of her friends because we read that faithful men have failed from among men. 'Fail' in Hebrew means 'to vanish'. Her friends have disappeared. The rapture having taken place, verses 2 through 5a picture defiant people rebelling against the Lord as evil flourishes. The church's restraint of evil being gone, wickedness abounds. Believe me, you do not want to be around when that time comes.

Scripture # 3:

Zephaniah 2:1-3

2:1 Gather yourselves together, yea, gather together, O nation not desired;

2 Before the decree bring forth, before the day pass as the chaff, before the fierce anger of the Lord come upon you, before the day of the Lord's anger come upon you.

3 Seek ye the Lord, all ye meek of the earth, which have wrought his judgment; seek righteousness, seek meekness: <u>it may be ye shall be **hid** in the day of the Lord's</u> anger.

Zephaniah pleads with people to seek the Lord through repentance before the 'Day of the Lord's' anger comes upon them. His cry is not to wait until it is too late to be hid from the day of God's wrath. Where will people be hidden? The Psalmist declares that God will hide His people *in the secret of His tabernacle* where He dwells [Psalms 27:5]. People hidden from

His indignation will be in heaven with Him abiding under the shadow of His wings [Psalms 91:1ff].

Notice also that people who escape the Lord's anger have humbled themselves with meekness [verse 3]. The Bible describes meekness as teachability in Psalms 25:9: *The meek will he guide in judgment; and the meek will he teach his way.* Therefore, believers who seek the Lord and are hidden from judgment are people who study the Bible in order to rightly divide it [2 Timothy 2:15]. They are rapture-ready; for they have searched the Scriptures in order to be *accounted worthy to escape all the things* that shall come upon the earth [Luke 21:36].

Before one can seek meekness to escape, however, a person must first seek righteousness. How is righteousness obtained? One becomes righteous by making Jesus his or her Lord. He is our righteousness when we receive Him as Savior. *Of him are ye in Christ Jesus, who of God is made unto us wisdom, and <u>righteousness</u>, and sanctification, and redemption* [1 Corinthians 1:30]. *For he hath made him to be sin for us, who knew no sin; that <u>we might be made</u> the <u>righteousness</u> of God in him* [2 Corinthians 5:21].

Have you put on Jesus' robe of righteousness? Have you asked God to forgive you of your sins? You do not have to name any of them because there is no way you could remember them all. So ask God to forgive you of all sin and He will. Make the confession out loud that you want Jesus to be Lord of your life. Confessing Jesus out loud lets satan and demons know Christ is now residing inside you giving you power of attorney to use Jesus' matchless name. You can do it this very moment if you are not yet saved. If you need help, read the chapter entitled 'How To Become A Christian'.

After making Jesus Lord, seek meekness by becoming teachable. Learn about the Lord through His Word. Be open to whatever it says. Do not take what others say as true until you prove it with Scripture. That includes me. This is the only way to keep from being deceived. Deception is the principal tactic of satan, and in the last days it will be extremely hard to discern truth as he promotes tolerance for all faiths as the highest virtue.   Deception is the primary way the devil impedes the power of God from flowing into the earth through believers who have the ability to stop his operations.

Scripture #4:

Isaiah 26:19-21
19 Thy dead men shall live, together with my dead body shall they arise. Awake and sing, ye that dwell in dust: for thy dew is as the dew of herbs, and <u>the earth shall cast out the dead</u>. (*Sleeping believers will be resurrected.*)

20 Come, my people (*living saints*), enter thou into thy chambers, and shut thy doors about thee: hide thyself as it were for a little moment, <u>until the indignation be overpast</u>. (*Believers raptured will miss the Tribulation.*)

21 For, behold, the Lord cometh out of his place to punish the inhabitants of the earth for their iniquity: the earth also shall disclose her blood, and shall no more cover her slain.

Hidden in this passage of Scripture is a prophecy about resurrection/rapture that Paul explains in his two letters to Thessaly. Remember how Paul told the Thessalonians in his first letter that the dead *in Christ shall arise first and then we who are alive and remain shall be caught up together with them to meet the Lord in the air*? Verse 19 above is an allusion to the dead rising first, and verse 20 speaks to those people caught up alive at the rapture. Old Testament Scriptures and New Testament Scriptures prophetically allign here.

Jesus was the Firstfruits of the resurrection [1 Corinthians 15:23]. After He arose from the dead, Matthew tells us that many people came up out of their graves and showed themselves to people in Jerusalem as having resurrected.

Matthew 27:52-53
52 And the graves were opened; and many bodies of the saints which slept arose,
53 And came out of the graves **after** his resurrection, and went into the holy city, and appeared unto many.

Why were the graves open? I suggest it was because they had to keep an appointment with Jesus. They became the wave sheaf of resurrected believers assuring a great harvest of resurrected souls at the end of the Church Age. This first cluster of resurrected believers corresponds to the Jewish ritual of waving before the Lord a bundle (called a sheaf) of the first pickings of the barley harvest at the Feast of Unleavened Bread as a thank offering in expectation of good harvests of every food type throughout the growing season.

According to the Essene calendar discovered among the Dead Sea Scrolls (DSS), the waving of a sheaf of barley was performed on the Sunday immediately following the first weekly Sabbath that occurred **after completing celebration** of the Feast of Unleavened Bread. For the record, this calendar does not correlate with the current Jewish calendar in use. Check the Internet for a comparison.

Firstfruits symbolizes the cream of any crop. Thus, Jesus along with the small group of resurrected believers mentioned only in the gospel of Matthew, signifies the firstfruits of God's people resurrected to life. Christ is the head, and the wave sheaf represents His body, the raptured Bride. The rest of the saints will be resurrected at the end of missionary activity when the Church Age is completed.

Every Man in His Own Order

The Bible teaches that the resurrection of saved people occurs in stages. Groups of saved believers will be resurrected in a God-ordained order according to Paul [1 Corinthians 15:23]. Jesus is the firstfruit and then comes the raptured Bride. Following will be the two witnesses at Midtrib as well as the 144,000 sealed Jewish saints who could conceivably be Jesus' honor guard throughout eternity. After this comes the general harvest of souls from the Grace Age, Tribulational martyrs, and old Testament believers. Jesus and His Bride resurrect before the Tribulation, but the other battalions resurrect during and at the end of the Tribulation.

Note the following verse in the book of Daniel:

Daniel 12:13
13 But go thou thy way [*Daniel*] till the **end** be: for thou shalt rest, and stand in thy lot at the end of the **days**.

Notice 'the end of the days' phrase. The angel had been talking to Daniel about Israel's future, about the 70-week prophecy Daniel was given in chapter 9. So the 'end of the days' is a reference to the end of the 490-years Jewish Age. Because Jesus is king, David is prophesied to be a prince over Israel during the Millennial Age [Ezekiel 34:23-24; 37:24-25]. Hence, Old Testament saints must have been resurrected at the end of the Age of Israel before the Millennial reign of Christ.

All these aforementioned groups comprise the first resurrection. The Bible writes *…blessed are they who take part in it* [Revelation 20:5, 6]. The people in this resurrection have names written in the Book of life. Every other person will resurrect after the Millennium Age is over. This is the 2nd resurrection to eternal death. At that time there will be a Great White Throne judgment of the works of people not written in the Book of Life [Revelation 20:11-15]. After that, God will create a new heaven and new earth wherein dwells righteousness forever.

Back to Isaiah's Prophecy…

In verse 20 of Isaiah 26 above, the prophet used the same word – 'come' – that John used when he penned Revelation 4:1. This intimates that the true church will be summoned to heaven through rapture to witness the coronation of King Jesus in heaven. Revelation chapters 4 and 5 is an account of Jesus' coronation.

When the parade of churches in chapters two and three of Revelation is ended, John is called to 'come up hither' [4:1]. Being the church's proxy in the vision, John's call to 'come up hither' symbolizes the church's seizure off earth. The three words are a clue telling us that Jesus' body of believers will be in heaven to witness King Jesus presented with the title of ownership and dominion of earth. After chapter five of Revelation, the church is not mentioned because her destiny has been fulfilled. Her betrothal will have been consummated, and she will witness Jesus' righteous claim to ownership of earth.

On earth, after rapture, things revert back to the Age of Israel and satan will again be in charge of earth without restraint because anointed believers will be gone. It will be the time of Jacob's trouble [Jeremiah 30:7], the final week of Israel's disciplinary punishment by the Lord. At the end of seven years, Jesus will with the words of His mouth end the Armageddon revolt against God, and the Kingdom of Heaven will begin its dominance over the planet.

In Isaiah 26:20 above, the church has entered her Bridegroom's chambers awaiting the time of return with her Lord to take over the world and reign. Notice the wording in verse twenty: *enter thou into thy chambers*, i.e., heaven, where the church is hidden. After entering, the doors are shut immediately until the *indignation is over*. Remember that 'indignation' is another term for God's wrath.

Once the church is raptured to heaven, no one else can come to the wedding ceremony because the doors are closed. This corresponds to the parable where five virgins of ten were not ready and could not go with the others to the wedding. Lamentably, while the unprepared virgins went to buy oil, the doors were shut.

Matthew 25:10-13

10 And while they went to buy, the bridegroom came; and they that were ready went in with him to the marriage: and the door was shut.

11 Afterward came also the other virgins, saying, Lord, Lord, open to us.

12 But he answered and said, Verily I say unto you, I know you not.

13 Watch therefore, for ye know neither the day nor the hour wherein the Son of man cometh.

According to the above, unprepared church people will have to endure the punishment of earth. *For, behold the Lord cometh out of his place to punish the inhabitants of the earth for their iniquity.* As Isaiah 26:21 alludes, this punishment is the very same hour of Tribulation that has been discussed in this essay.

Conclusion

Other Scriptures could be presented which indicate rapture precedes Tribulation; but ample evidence has been given to convince a reasonable person that believing Christians can comfort themselves regarding this imminent event called rapture.

Biblical proof is overwhelming that Antichrist will never put his mark on the Bride of Christ because she will be gone before he comes on the scene to make his bid to rule the world. He is probably alive today, but he cannot come forth to rule until believers are raptured off earth.

Since the world stage is set for the last act of the times of the gentiles as per Ezekiel chapters 38 and 39, I exhort you to keep looking up for the appearance of our Lord to seize us out of here and take us to the glorious celestial city of God, the New Jerusalem [Hebrews 12:22]. I submit that the message of a Tribulation period is not one of doom and gloom for rapturites but rather a message heralding consummation of our hope of glory.

The Bible repeatedly warns that sin has consequences and to teach otherwise would be to promote error. The coming judgment of God on sin and eternal damnation awaiting Christ rejectors are Bible truths. We cannot ignore them. We can, however, rejoice in the fact that true believers in the family of God who are rapture-ready will escape all the forthcoming righteous judgments of a sin-sick world.

Without a genuine a lie is not possible; therefore, an imitation is the sincerest proof of authenticity. Hence, the masquerading New World Order of the Antichrist will be crushed and blown away by the emerging New World Order of the Kingdom of God.

The fabricated globalist Order of 2520 precise days will be short-lived. Jesus Himself affirmed the crushing of this newly ordered system in His Olivet Discourse. And He further urged His disciples to keep themselves worthy to escape the tribulations that birth His Kingdom.

Not only will the restraint on humanity's sinful nature be removed in the Tribulation exposing the depths of human depravity, but also *heavenly bodies shall be shaken* (causing men to) *faint from terror, apprehensive of the anguish and perplexity that is coming on the world* [Luke 21:25, 26 (NIV)].

Are you Rapture-Ready?

CHAPTER -6

RECAPITULATION CONFIRMS RAPTURE A WORTHY GOAL

Many people believe that the church will go through the seven years of Tribulation either part way or all the way. They try to shame and intimidate those of us who do not accept that teaching by saying that Pretribulationists have an escape mentality which is ignoble and misguided. Their logic is faulty as has been shown in the previous chapters. Our Lord Jesus Himself cautioned His disciples that escaping those days was a valuable reward granted to people who merit it, to honorable people worthy enough to be gloriously taken away from the awful judgmental days of woe. Let me repeat what He said in the Olivet Discourse:

Luke 21:36
36 Watch ye therefore, and pray always, that ye may be accounted worthy to escape all these things that shall come to pass, and to stand before the Son of man.

It is clear from the above that our Lord wants His people to be diligent in keeping themselves rapture-ready. Why did He say it was a worthy goal? I submit it is because the Day of the Lord's wrath on sin will be unbelievably horrendous such that no flesh would survive – like in the worldwide flood of Genesis – if

God in His mercy does not shorten the days. Thank God, He will in mercy shorten them [Matthew 24:21, 22].

That seven-year time period spoken by Daniel the prophet is prophetically sealed to contain an exact number of 2,520 days plus 75 extra days at the end [Daniel 12:7-13]. Since God has spoken and it cannot be changed, I believe Jesus meant that somehow God is going to actually shorten daytime and darkness at some point in the Tribulation in order for the populace to pass through that period faster than otherwise would be the case.

Could that actually happen? Yes, it can. Remember when Joshua commanded the sun and moon to stand still and the Lord hearkened unto his words?

Joshua 10:12-14

12 Then spake Joshua to the Lord in the day when the Lord delivered up the Amorites before the children of Israel, and he said in the sight of Israel, Sun, stand thou still upon Gibeon; and thou, Moon, in the valley of Ajalon.

13 And **the sun stood still, and the moon stayed**, until the people had avenged themselves upon their enemies. Is not this written in the book of Jasher? So the sun stood still in the midst of heaven, and hasted not to go down <u>about a whole day</u>.

14 And there was no day like that before it or after it, that the Lord hearkened unto the voice of a man: <u>for the Lord fought for Israel</u> (*with astronomical weaponry*).

We know from Joshua's victorious challenge to cosmological routine, the day was lengthened by the space of about a whole day. Evidence in astronomical calculations using computers shows that indeed a day is missing in charting heavenly bodies backwards. I have read that the earth's tilt has been changed by a few degrees at some point in time. If so, this could account for a longer daytime in one hemisphere and a longer nighttime in the opposite.

Weirdly but fittingly, records exist in China which report that at about the time of Joshua, there was a day when the nighttime was almost twice as long as usual. Given this anomaly of a long day and long night, could not God shorten days as is prophesied for the Tribulation? God can change natural phenomenological events to suit His purposes. After all, He created everything. He has merely to speak a Word, and everything harmoniously changes without catastrophic annihilation. That is how He created. *He spoke and it was done* [Psalms 33:6, 9].

I believe that Joshua's supernatural disturbance of the natural order of things was a type of an antitype[1], both of which respond to a superimposition of spiritual intervention to rearrange physical laws. It will happen again in the Day of the Lord's wrath. The last part of verse 14 of Joshua 10 above says *...the Lord fought for Israel.* Who but God can command heavenly bodies to obey, and they obey?

Amazingly, the sun and moon became Joshua's strategic armor to oust the remaining seven of the ten strongest nations inhabiting Canaan. Three of the ten nations had already been defeated by Israel with supernatural help from God. But the battle in which the sun and moon stood still was the definitive battle requiring extra daylight to rout the remaining seven partnering Canaanite nations; and it foreshadows the last battle

---

[1] A type is a figure, representation, or symbol of something to come, such as an event in the Old Testament that foreshadows another event to come. Types and antitypes abound in Scripture. They are real events prophetic or predictive of a similar real event in future time teaching spiritual truths with physical sensory paraphernalia. Ordinarily the type is a portrayal on a lesser scale of the antitype.

of the Armageddon campaign composed of a United Nations allied force coming against Israel at the end of the Tribulation. Although the time is different, the battlefield is the same – the plain of Megiddo in Israel.

When this long day of Joshua's battle was over, the Hebrews fought smaller skirmishes to dislodge the remaining people left in pockets throughout the land. Joshua's battle was a type of Armageddon when Jesus comes to overthrow the unholy trinity – satan, the false prophet, and the Antichrist – along with their armies after which Jesus will take over and rule the world [Revelation 19:11-16].

True to the type, Jesus will fight for Israel and defeat their enemies with the Word of His mouth like Joshua did. Meteorite showers of huge boulder-sized hail (around 100 pounds each [Revelation 16:21]) will supernaturally demolish Antichrist's armies in like manner as happened in Joshua's battle [Joshua 10:11].

Joshua is the English equivalent of the Hebrew word Yeshua meaning Savior. So, Joshua saved the Israelite warriors with His words invoking the sun and moon's help after which they took over the land of Palestine God gave them – the type. Jesus will similarly save the Israelites with His Words in the Tribulation and will take over not just Palestine but the whole world – the antitype.

Kept From the Hour Guarantees a Rapture

One of the clearest passages of Scripture explaining that rapture is a blessed event promised to the faithful in Christ is the following:

Revelation 3:10-11

10 Because thou hast kept the word of my patience, I also will keep thee from the hour of temptation which shall come upon all the world, to try them that dwell upon the earth.

11 Behold, I come quickly: hold that fast which thou hast, that no man take thy crown.

The above promise in verse 10 that Jesus gave to the Philadelphian church in the book of Revelation is accompanied by a warning in verse 11 to hold fast to your faith that Jesus will suddenly snatch His Bride off the planet. The words in verse ten could not be any clearer. The *hour of temptation* is the seven-year Tribulation when God judges sin in the world. It is satan's final hour to have jurisdiction over the whole earth. God permits him to show his true colors and character, for he is not an angel of light [2 Corinthians 11:13-15].

In the parade of churches mentioned in Revelation chapters two and three, Philadelphia is next to last. As mentioned before, Jesus prophesies that the last church, Laodicea, would be lukewarm and compromising causing Him to vomit it up. How nauseous worldliness must be to our Lord. Like the church in Sardis, this last church had no commendation as the other five had, only castigation because of their lack of awareness concerning their spiritual condition.

On the other hand, Jesus highly esteems the Philadelphian church. Having struggled out of the death grip of the Sardis church, Philadelphians are zealous to get the gospel message out to the world. The era that this church depicts started around the 17th century when missionary activity began to escalate due to a series of great revivals, the American War for Independence, and the Industrial Revolution.

All church eras depicted in Revelation overlap. Each church's mystique exists in some measure within the universal church all the way up to the termination of the Church Age. Looking backward in time one sees a progressive enlightenment of Jesus' body of believers through the Age of Grace, and this development reflects the spirit of each church.

Philadelphians and Laodiceans dwell side-by-side until the rapture. After rapture, the Laodiceans continue into Tribulation while true born-again prepared church believers represented by Philadelphia <u>escape</u> to heaven and miss the awful time of trouble that will try, test, or purify earth-dwellers [verse 10].

Rapture Proved By A Two Letter Greek Pronoun

Verse ten of Revelation three reads…I *will keep thee <u>FROM</u> the hour of temptation.* Notice the English preposition 'from' translating the Greek preposition *ek* meaning 'out of'. The Greek *ek tes hora* literally reads, '<u>out of</u> the midst of the hour' or to paraphrase, 'clean away from the hour or time set for Tribulation'.

A student of Greek reports that the Greek preposition *ek* <u>NEVER</u> means 'to stay within'. In Spiros Zodhiates' Complete Word Study of the New Testament, the pronoun usage for the following prepositions in phrases are:

- *Eis – to enter into*
- *En – to remain within*
- *Ek – to take out of.*

Used over 800 times in the New Testament, I understand that only once is *ek* improperly rendered.

Another instance where pronoun usage can be misleading is in the gospel message of salvation. Galatians 3:8 reads that God justifies or makes righteous the heathen 'through' faith, but it is not our natural faith which many people erroneously think. Salvation is 'by' Jesus' supernatural faith in His Father's plan of redemption.

Isaiah 53:11 tells us that it is '...*by Jesus' knowledge that He justifies many...*' meaning that Jesus knew what He was doing when He went to the cross and obeyed the Father's plan. His faith in trusting His Father to resurrect Him from hell is the gift given to us as the book of Ephesians teaches.

Ephesians 2:8

8 For by grace are ye saved through (*the channel*) faith; and **that** (*the faith*) not of yourselves: it is the gift of God:

The above preposition 'through' is in Greek *dia* which signifies the channel through which something comes. The referent of 'that' is the faith through which salvation is given. So, faith is a gift of God given to us, and the gift is Jesus' faith. Read it again...

Ephesians 2:8

8 For by grace you have been saved through faith. And **that** (*the faith*) is the gift of God, **not** your faith *(that causes salvation. You merely respond by receiving the gift.)*

Paul stated the same thing in his letter to Galatians when he said,

Galatians 2:16

16 Knowing that a man is not justified by the works of the law, but by the faith OF Jesus Christ, even we have believed in Jesus Christ, that we might be justified by the faith OF Christ, and not by the works of the law: for by the

works of the law shall no flesh be justified. (*Twice it states justification is by Jesus' faith, not ours*)

Moreover,

Galatians 2:20

20 I am crucified with Christ: nevertheless I live; yet not I, but Christ liveth in me: and the life which I now live in the flesh <u>I live by the faith **OF** the Son of God</u>, who loved me, and gave himself for me.

If it is Jesus' faith with which we believers move mountains (problems), how can we fail? Can God fail? Absolutely not; so I submit we fail for lack of knowledge [Hosea 4:6]. Therefore, I exhort the reader to receive the Revelation in 3:10 which clearly promises that Jesus will come for His rapture-ready Bride in order to take her out of the middle of the process whereby God judges sinful earth-dwellers.

Mid- and Posttribulationists say the entire church will go <u>through</u> Tribulation. Some teach that the true church of born-again people will be protected while earth is cleansed by fire; others say the church will partake of the hour to suffer purging. Those are clear refutations of the meaning of the Greek preposition *ek*.

For example:

- *<u>Out of</u> Egypt have I called My Son* [Matthew 2:15].
- *First cast out the beam <u>out of</u> thine own eye* [Matthew 7:5].
- *...For <u>out of</u> the heart proceed evil thoughts* [Matthew 15:19].
- *And many bodies of the saints came <u>out of</u> the graves after His resurrection* [Matthew 27:53].

- *I will spew thee __out of__ My mouth* [Revelation 3:16].

- *Etc.*

Kept Out of What?

The Scripture we have been analyzing is a plain and unambiguous testimony to the fact that rapture precedes Tribulation. Why is it so important that rapture comes first? I will answer with a question. From what are Jesus' faithful witnesses being kept? They are kept *from __the__ hour of __the__ temptation* (or testing).

The word 'the' preceding 'hour' and 'temptation' is in grammar a definite article meaning a particular one or the only one. This hour and this temptation are special, two distinct concepts without duplication. Nothing could be more special than the 7-year Tribulation period that terminates in open manifestation of the glorious Kingdom of Heaven on earth.

The reason the hour is called a temptation or testing is because the seven-year Tribulation constitutes the Days of Awe when men must decide whether they will make Christ or the Antichrist their Lord. They will be tested to see to whom they will show allegiance when presented with the choice of whether to take the mark of the beast. It is the same test Adam and Eve faced.

Because the Philadelphians have not forsaken the true doctrines about Jesus' death, burial, and resurrection, because they have carried that gospel message to the far corners of the earth, and because they have *purified themselves,* God plans to keep them __from__ the Day of His vengeance upon sin by taking them 'out of' the wrath to come.

God foreordained them to rapture before the world began because He knew the Philadelphians would choose not to deny His name or His Word in spite of intimidation to defect the apostolic doctrines of a rapture and a Millennial Kingdom. As in the days of Noah and Lot, God will deliver His faithful followers 'out of' harm's way.

The Wrath of God or The Wrath of satan?

Revelation 6:17
17 For the great day of his wrath is come; and who shall be able to stand?

According to the above verse, the great day of God's wrath starts in chapter six verse seventeen of John's Apocalypse. Chapter six wherein are the seals to the title deed of earth is in my opinion a panorama of the entire seven-year Tribulation and acts like a Table of Contents for the coming judgments outlined in Revelation.

The seven seals forecast what the book is about for this chapter quickly gives one a pithy synopsis of what will transpire throughout the whole period. So, from chapters six through nineteen, all events are included as a part of the day of God's wrath even though there may be a short respite between the difficult ordeals plaguing men.

Remember that the Bible describes Tribulation as a woman travailing to deliver a baby. Pains begin comparatively mild and slowly escalate to excruciatingly hard labor right before the baby emerges. Similarly, the Tribulation period mirrors the birthing process as the Kingdom of Heaven hidden in the hearts of believers for almost 2,000 years comes forth.

A child of God never suffers the wrath of God. Any suffering endured is self-induced. What happens is that a believer removes himself out from under God's protective covering due to broken fellowship caused by persistent sin. Note how the Bible states it: *Fools because of their transgressions, and because of their iniquities, are afflicted* [Psalms 107:17]. They bring upon themselves satanic harassment because when one conceives sin by obeying the devil's temptations, satan becomes the sinner's onerous lord till they repent.

Romans 6:16

16 Know ye not, that to whom ye yield yourselves servants to obey, his servants ye are to whom ye obey; whether of sin unto death, or of obedience unto righteousness?

God's children often open doors to satan's wrath but never to God's wrath. Satan's wrath is not the same as God's pent up final fury poured out during the Tribulation. His anger will involve extraordinary cosmological disturbances even planetary conflicts over which satan has no control.

Archangel Michael Stands Down in the Tribulation

When God removes His protective restraint upon sin in the Tribulation, God will allow satan to have a field day in bringing the world to its destructive end. The Almighty will let people experience what it is like living with satan as their god without hindrance. Israel's tribal prince the archangel Michael, whom God commissioned to protect them from the devil's efforts to annihilate them so that they could not bring forth a Kinsman-Redeemer, will <u>stand down</u> from his unseen protective role guarding Israel's welfare.

Daniel 12:1

1 And at that time shall Michael <u>stand up</u>, the great prince which standeth for the children of thy people: and

there shall be a time of trouble, such as never was since there was a nation even to that same time: and at that time thy people shall be delivered, every one that shall be found written in the book.

Jesus referred to the above Scripture when He spoke about the horrendous times of the Tribulation in His Olivet Discourse. Never will there be a time again such as earth-dwellers will experience. The verse above reports that Michael will 'stand up' at that time implying he will protect the Hebrews from assault by Antichrist. However, I submit that translation is misleading.

The Hebrew word used for 'stand up' is *amad,* and it means 'to rise up', 'to take a stand', or 'to remain motionless'. Motionless assumes the sense of 'to cease' or to 'stop doing something'. In my estimation, this sense fits the context better. The end of the previous chapter along with this verse is talking about God's endtime Day of Vengeance on sin for which Daniel wrote the Scripture. This is the era which births the Kingdom of God.

We have learned God allows Israel to be scourged due to her continual flagrant disobedience in spurning God's attempts to draw her to Him. Therefore, Michael will 'stand down', not 'up', from protecting God's elect people because it is the time of Jacob's trouble to birth the Kingdom Age. God wants them to experience the horror of being without supernatural help when Michael stands motionless during the scourge of satan's wrath terrorizing them.

God published through prophecy that Israel would *receive of the Lord's hand double for all her sins* [Isaiah 40:2]. Prophecy also indicates that God would especially judge her harshly for rejecting and killing His promised Messiah. Because Scripture prophesies that the Hebrews will go through a second holocaust worse than the one they experienced in World War II, the powerful Michael must refrain from his protection of God's elect nation. Therefore, I submit that a better translation of the above King James Bible quote is...

Daniel 12:1

1   At that time shall Michael stand down motionless, the great prince God ordained to protect God's people from enemy harassment; and there shall be a time of trouble never before experienced nor ever shall be again; and at that time only the people ordained to populate the Millennial Kingdom will be protected by Michael in the mountains of Jordan from tribulation.

(Paraphrased by author)

Note that **only** the few Jews chosen by God to populate the Kingdom Age after the Tribulation will be protected in the mountains of Jordan from the bane of Antichrist [Matthew 24:15, 16]. Thus, Michael will stand down (motionless) for all others.

God's wrath will be evidenced in allowing satan the father of sin to show forth his heinous ability to plague men. As Tribulation progresses, the Almighty's indignation escalates as He permits people who rejected His mercy and grace before rapture to be plagued and tortured by evil demonic creatures loosed from the abyss, creatures that have been pent up until the day of judgment on sin [Revelation 9:14-21].

Finally, the unfolding of cosmological turmoil only God can perform will compound the woes upon earth during satan's reign of terror through the Antichrist. The last threshold of God's wrath, the extremely devastating bowl judgments, will probably be the time when He shortens the days or no flesh would survive. Are you worthy to escape the 'Days of Awe'?

Are you Rapture-Ready?

CHAPTER -7

DAY OF DESTINY

Biblicists for the most part promote the notion that we cannot know the date of the rapture. They say this because Jesus said we would not know the day or the hour of our miraculous departure to heaven. Because there are twenty-four time zones around the earth, it is true that the day and hour for everyone on the planet is different. But, does that preclude not knowing the date?

From Daniel's 70 Weeks Prophecy, the Pharisees, Sadducees, priests, scribes, and rulers in Israel should have known the very day Jesus would present Himself to His people as their Messiah King. They were expecting Messiah but were unsure Jesus was him. Since they should have known He was the one via the Tanakh, and since John-the-Baptist said He was the one, Jesus chastised them for not acknowledging He was the one about whom the Scriptures spoke.

Old Testament prophecies pointed out that Jesus was Messiah at His first appearance. Given there are eight times as many prophecies about His return, let's see if we can determine from Scriptural types and shadows whether Jesus is ready to fulfill prophecies about His 2nd Advent. Determination involves examining what Jesus meant when He said the day and hour is unknown for His return.

Mark 13:32-37

32 But of that day and that hour knoweth no man, no, not the angels which are in heaven, neither the Son, but the Father.

33 Take ye heed, WATCH$_1$ and pray: for ye know not when the time is.

34 For **the Son** of Man is as a man taking a far journey, who left his house, and gave authority to his servants, and to every man his work, and **commanded** the porter to WATCH$_2$.

35 WATCH$_3$ ye therefore: for ye know not when the master of the house cometh, at even, or at midnight, or at the cockcrowing, or in the morning:

36 Lest **coming suddenly** he find you sleeping.

37 And what I say unto you I say unto all, WATCH$_4$.

It is clear from the above that the Son wants His people to watch (spoken 4 times) and does not want anyone to know the exact time (verse 32). Why? If known, people would put off watching until just before the day arrives thinking they have time to repent and to clean up their act. Hence, unpreparedness in holiness will thrust many people into the Tribulation.

Jesus said several times that we would not know the day and hour for rapture, but He never did say we could not know the timing. What's the difference? Apostle Paul implied that being children of the day we would know the times and the seasons of Jesus' return to snatch us off earth because we will have been watching and realize the nearness of the Day of the Lord [1 Thessalonians 5:1-9].

The rapture happens in context with the sudden appearance of the Day of the Lord which births the Kingdom of Heaven. When a woman is pregnant, it is obvious; and the closer to the appearance of the baby, the more obvious it is. Nonetheless, no matter how obvious, the exact day and hour of a baby's birth is unknown. All anyone can do, even the mother, is to watch, wait, and stay ready for the birth. I believe Jesus likened the day-and-hour to the critical moment a baby separates from the birth canal.

Apostle Paul's Account of the 'Day of Destiny'

1 Thessalonians 5:1, 4-6

1 But of the times and the seasons, brethren, ye have no need that I write unto you...

4 But ye, brethren, are not in darkness, that **THAT** day should overtake you as a thief. (*When you are in the season, <u>watch</u> how pregnant the time gets.*)

5 Ye are all the <u>children of light</u>, and the <u>children of the day</u>: we are not of the night, nor of darkness.

6 Therefore let us not sleep, as do others; but <u>let us watch</u> and be sober.

Paul asserts that so long as we keep constantly watching as Jesus commands in the gospels, our 'Day of Destiny' would not come upon us as a thief as verse 4 implies. Closer inspection of all Jesus and Apostle Paul said about the timing of His return, reveals that IT IS POSSIBLE to know when the clock will strike midnight. But it takes close inspection and great belief to flow upstream against the view that it is not possible.

In the march of the Church Age in Revelation chapters 2 and 3 of the Apocalypse churches, Sardis, being a middle church, metaphorically represented the close of the thousand-years Dark Ages.   Notice what Jesus said to the dead church in Sardis in Revelation chapter 3 verse 3 below. She had been dead for a long time because the Bible had been hidden under the altars of the church by the clergy. But God still loves her and is coaxing her to repent so as not to miss rapture.

Jesus warned Sardis to strengthen what little doctrinal truth remained [verse 2 below] so that the few remnant believers in the city who were *watching* and keeping their garments clean might know by current events when the time was at hand for Jesus' return. This is a veiled appeal to believers today to hold fast to the sound doctrine received in the church's first-century existence. But the warning to repent is not veiled. It is sound advice to turn away from the doctrines of error that have corrupted the church and have caused her to apostatize. It is an appeal to return to preaching the bloody cross.

Revelation 3:2-3
2 Be watchful, and strengthen the things which remain, that are ready to die: for I have not found thy works perfect before God.
3 Remember therefore how thou hast received and heard, and hold fast, and repent. **IF** therefore thou shalt not WATCH, I will come on thee <u>as a thief</u>, and thou shalt <u>not know what hour</u> I will come upon thee.

Note the word "if" in verse 3 for it signifies the possibility that a believer <u>could know </u>the hour Jesus comes to snatch away His Bride from the period of turmoil. But it is contingent upon one watching and thus knowing by the signs on earth and the signals in heaven that the Kingdom Age is near to be born. The worse things become on earth, the darker more corrupt and violent men become, the more we can know that heaven is about to open its doors for Jesus' glorious Bride.

Only after the rapture will we have proof positive of the date that all heaven has been waiting for – the marriage of the Lamb of God. However, in each of the actual raptures reported in the Bible typifying the church's rapture, the participants knew in advance that they would be going to heaven. Let's look at three rapture events recorded in the Scriptures that have occurred.

Enoch was translated that he should not see death according to Hebrews 11:5. We know from Enoch's book that when he visited heaven in open visions, he learned that he was going to stay there one day and not return to earth. Likewise, Elijah, Elisha, and the School of the Prophets knew in advance Elijah was going to be taken to heaven without dying [2 Kings 2:1-12].

Our Lord Jesus also knew He was going to ascend to heaven in rapture 40 days after His resurrection. This is now celebrated as Ascension Day. He tarried around the earth forty days talking to His disciples about the Kingdom of Heaven in preparation for their work on earth. *He commanded them to preach unto the people and to testify that it is he which was ordained of God to be the Judge of the quick* (living) *and dead* [Acts 10:42].

So, after Jesus exhorted His disciples for forty days, the new Age of Grace began. Ten days after He ascended was Pentecost at which time Jesus and the Father planned to send the Holy Spirit to indwell believers. Why was the Holy Spirit sent? Christians need Him for power to witness about Jesus' eternality and Godhood [John 15:26 and Acts 1:8].

If the head of the church knew the time of His departure to heaven, and if the Old Testament types knew theirs, it stands to reason that the people making up Christ's body ought to know when they would ascend to the head and complete the body of Christ.

Recapitulation of Jesus' Words about Sardis

Revelation 3:1-3

1 ...thou hast a name that thou livest, and art dead.

2 Be <u>WATCHFUL</u>, and strengthen the things which remain, that are ready to die: for I have not found thy works perfect before God.

3 Remember therefore how thou hast received and heard, and hold fast, and REPENT. <u>If therefore thou shalt not watch,</u> I will come on thee as a thief, and <u>thou shalt not know</u> what hour I will come upon thee.

When giving instructions to the people of Sardis, Jesus admonished them to remember their first teachings – the original gospel of the Blood for salvation and the following glory of Holy Spirit power to testify regarding the credentials of Jesus as Messiah. He told them to hold fast to the gospel they first heard, i.e., to preaching the bloody cross. They were to repent for neglecting to make it the central message in every sermon because without the blood there is no Eternal Life. Working for God's favor by performing good deeds is the reason Jesus said that the Sardis church was dead with little or no life left within it.

Eternal Life Comes by Faith and Not Works

The Sardinian church died because its citizenry were relying on their good works for salvation rather than resting by faith in the finished work of Jesus on the cross. The Reformation helped in part to correct doctrinal errors that were killing the church. But sadly, the religious errors are alive and well today.

Current preaching about self-aggrandizement, self-esteem, self-enhancement, success and achievement has caused the contemporary church to become unmoored again from its original mandate of only preaching the good news of the mercy of the cross without any works added. Today, preaching has been focused primarily on building temporal personal kingdoms rather than the Kingdom of God.

The aphorism that the work of the cross is so magnificent we can't even leave a tip is a terse summary of salvation. Yet pastors have inadvertently urged their flocks to pray more, study more, give more, do whatever more to be blessed, which beclouds the riches of God's grace in so great a free salvation as the cross of Calvary provides.

How does one take up his own cross and please God as Luke says we should do [Luke 9:23]? God is pleased when we crucify our flesh and separate from the world. ...*Friendship of the world is enmity with God*... [James 4:4]. But sadly, worldliness has defaced Christian distinctives and uprooted its purity. Like Ephesus, Sardis and New Age Christianity have left their first love.

Deification of self a la humanism, produces a performance-based spirituality, and the New Age ecumenical retreat from Protestantism back to Catholicism has caused the modern Sardinian church to become twice dead [Jude 12] – once dead by physical birth with a sin nature, and dead the second time by retreating from salvation by grace, by backsliding into the Old Testament's works-based system for salvation.

Back to Our Quest...

What is almost hidden in verse 3 above is the veiled concept that believers who are not hell-bound, who watch and strengthen the truth by not blurring or confusing it with mixed heathenistic practices, can know the sudden and unexpected hour Jesus will come back for His Bride as a thief. Did you get that? Believers can know the time!

Jesus counsels Sardinians that if they are <u>NOT</u> watching, He would sneak up on their blind side as a thief, and people would see that they were nude and disrobed of their righteous garments. Therefore, whoever refuses to get excited enough to research Jesus' numerous calls to watch and be rapture-ready, is at risk of being left behind at rapture because of being stripped naked of their garment of righteousness without which no one will enter heaven.

Revelation 16:15
15 Behold, I come as a thief. Blessed is he that watcheth, and keepeth his garments, lest he walk naked, and they see his shame.

Note how our Lord lectures Sardis in Revelation 3:3. Go back and read it again. <u>NOT</u> to watch means you will <u>NOT</u> know the hour He comes. But the reverse obtains too. If you <u>are</u> <u>watching</u> and paying attention to the scriptures and aligning them with the signals of heaven, such as the recent tetrad total lunar eclipses happening on the four feast days of Passover and Tabernacles in years 2014 and 2015 and the Star of Bethlehem's reoccurrence after 2,000 years throughout the year 2021, you

<u>can know the hour</u> Jesus will step through the threshold of heaven.

Is not Jesus' admonition to the Sardinians an invitation to seek for clues signifying rapture so that 1) we are not naked regarding His hour of power and 2) that He does not come when we are not expecting Him?

At Jesus' First Advent, the Pharisees and scribes could have known through the book of Daniel the very day Jesus presented Himself as Messiah in the Temple [Mark 11:2-11]. John the Baptist had identified Him as the Lamb of God [John 1:29, 36], God's Anointed One, which is the reason Jesus chastened His people for not heeding what they had heard from prophet John. May the Lord not chasten us as well for being ignorant of the rapture date at the Bema Seat of Christian judgment.

Sudden Destruction

Having discussed the importance of watching while awaiting the Lord's return, let's find out how watching will keep us protected from ensnarement brought about by sudden destruction, how preparedness for rapture shields one from becoming a prey to catastrophe during the time of Jacob' trouble [Jeremiah 30:7].

Previous chapters have noted that believers looking for the Blessed Hope, Jesus Christ [Titus 2:13], will be swiftly snatched away from Tribulation by a sudden explosive radiation blast. In studying the Shroud of Turin's imprint of Jesus' resurrection on His burial cloth, I have learned that the marks on the cloth were those of a crucified man from Jerusalem and were made by an explosive radiation blast, a flash of light that man is incapable of producing because it requires equipment and power outside man's capability to develop. Search the Internet and see for yourself because it is an interesting report of scientists from Italy.

Considering that Jesus was awakened by a lightning-like blast of radiation, and considering the adage – like father, like son, – we can surmise that since Jesus, the church's head was resurrected by a flash of radiation, so will His body of born-again believers be captured into heaven by irradiation [1 Thessalonians 4:17].

A Deeper Probe of the Evidence of Rapture

In the Greek language, as in Hebrew, there were neither chapter divisions nor verses in the early church era when the New Testament was written. This means that chapter 5 of First Thessalonians is a continuation of the thematic context of the last verses of chapter 4 wherein we are informed that the Bride will meet Jesus in the air at the 'great snatch'. Let's examine again the connecting words of the passage.

The very first word of verse 1 is the conjunction 'but' which connects chapter 5 to 4. Even verses 2 and 3 start off with 'for', another connecting word revealing the continuation of the ending concept of chapter 4 about rapture. Why is it important to connect the two chapters? It is for the reason that the sudden destruction of verse 3 in chapter 5 which starts with the Day of the Lord seems tied to the sudden departure of the church in the last part of chapter 4. By probing a little deeper, we find that they tie together the 'Day of Destiny' for all earth-dwellers.

1 Thessalonians 4:17

17 Then we which are alive and remain shall be caught up together with them in the clouds, to meet the Lord in the air: and so shall we ever be with the Lord.

1 Thessalonians 5:1-4

1 But of the times and the seasons, brethren, <u>ye</u> have no need that I write unto <u>you</u>.

2 For yourselves know perfectly that the day of the Lord so cometh as a thief in the night.

3 For when <u>they</u> shall say, Peace and safety; then SUDDEN DESTRUCTION cometh upon <u>them</u>, as travail upon a woman with child; and they shall not escape.

4 But <u>ye</u>, brethren, are not in darkness, that that day should overtake <u>you</u> as a thief.

Notice that all four of the verses in chapter 5 begin with connecting words that imply a continuation of the thought about the rapture mentioned at the end of chapter 4. The first person pronouns change to third person pronouns in verse 3. For this reason, we can rightfully deduce that the children of light (the 'ye' and 'you') who are watching for the rapture event will escape the sudden destruction that comes upon all other (the 'they' and 'them') earth-dwellers.

The inference of <u>escape</u> by the church and <u>sudden destruction</u> of others suggests a concomitant, affiliated, or related event by the two groups of people. Does related mean that the two events concerning the pronoun change happen on the same day?

From the above, it seems like the ideas of rapture and sudden destruction are inseparable. They appear to be woven together happening simultaneously or so close as to appear to be one event on the same day. Here is what Luke says about the Day of the Lord:

Luke 21:34-36
34 And take heed to yourselves, lest at any time your hearts be overcharged with surfeiting, and drunkenness, and cares of this life, and so that day [*the Day of the Lord*] come upon you unawares.
35 For AS A SNARE shall it come on ALL them that dwell on the face of the WHOLE earth.
36 Watch ye therefore, and pray always, that ye may be accounted worthy to escape all these things that shall come to pass, and to stand before the Son of man.

The 'Day of Destiny' will come upon all earth-dwellers – some to escape and all others to entrapment in the Tribulational period. In the Luke 21 passage, Jesus talks about the fig leaf generation experiencing '*that day*' which comes upon the whole world. Most scholars agree that modern Israel is the fig leaf generation which has sprouted. Jesus forewarned that generation would live to see the birthing of the Kingdom of Heaven on earth.

So, it appears like the only way to escape the snare set for the whole world is to make the rapture, to join the Philadelphian church track and stay off the Laodicean track [Revelation 3:7ff]. And as verse 36 in Luke 21 above warns, the criteria to be found worthy enough to escape the great Tribulation is to watch and to pray always. Don't let anyone rob you of your blessed hope of rapture.

Do we have Biblical witnesses that the rapture and sudden destruction happen at the same time? Four precedents in the Old Testament are harbingers or types of what is to come that relate to the concept that the 'Day of Destiny' will ensnare all people.

Typology

The Old Testament is loaded with typology. As has been noted, a type is an example or pattern forecasting what will happen in a similar manner later. In the Old Testament, the type acts as a shadow symbolizing through representation on a small scale what will happen in the future on a larger scale. It attests to the maxim that the Old Testament is the New Testament concealed and the New Testament is the Old Testament revealed. Let's look at some examples.

Example #1 – Noah's Flood

We know from Genesis 7 that when Noah entered the ark, the worldwide flood came upon all the earth and caught everyone but Noah and his family by surprise. You will discover that in all four types, the people who did not escape judgment were destroyed because they did not expect to be caught by sudden destruction. Indeed, Noah preached 120 years warning about the corruption of his day, but they would not hear and repent. Thus, the zeitgeist (spirit) of the time – violence and corruption – brought forth the cleansing flood.

Jesus Himself contrasted the accompanying suddenness of escape for one group of people with the suddenness of destruction of another group of people. Was it coincidentally at the same time? The Genesis account reports that God shut the doors to Noah's ark Himself. And Jesus clarified that they were shut on the same day the rains began. Jesus is speaking here....

Luke 17:27

27 They did eat, they drank, they married wives, they were given in marriage, until <u>THE DAY that Noe entered into the ark</u>, and THE FLOOD CAME, and DESTROYED them all.

Noah and his family escaped destruction by entering the safe haven of the ark God told him to build. Amazingly, after preaching about unrighteousness and the need for repentance for 120 years, only 8 people were saved even though anyone who believed the message of Noah that judgment was coming could have entered the ark and been saved. This is the first example of sudden destruction for one group and escape for another group happening on the same day.

Example #2 – Sodom's Destruction

In the account of Lot's escape from Sodom in Genesis 19:20, Lot asked the angels who were guiding him to safety for permission to go <u>**up**</u> to a small city in the mountains called Zoar. The Biblical narrative says that the angels were in a hurry to protect him from the imminent volcanic eruption. They gave permission for Lot to go up **QUICKLY** for nothing could be done till *<u>righteous</u>* Lot [2 Peter 2:6-8] was safely out of harm's way. Is this incident forecasting that the *<u>righteous</u>* church, the *repentant* prepared church making up the chosen Bride, must be gone before the 'Day of Destiny' happens – the 'Day of the Lord's' judgmental wrath?

Going <u>up</u> to the city of Zoar on the mountain corresponds to Noah being elevated <u>up</u> above the waters of destruction. Both Noah and Lot demonstrated that escape was <u>upward</u> as is escape for rapturites who will be caught <u>up</u> into the air as per 1 Thessalonians 4:17. But the important thing for our purpose here is that escape and destruction happened the same day. Let's hear Jesus again mention this fact in the Lot narrative.

Luke 17:28-29

28 Likewise also as it was in the days of Lot; they did eat, they drank, they bought, they sold, they planted, they builded;

29 But THE SAME DAY that Lot went out of Sodom it rained fire and brimstone from heaven, and destroyed them all. [*Lot escaped but Sodomites burned.*]

Example #3 – Jericho and Rachel

In chapter 6 of Joshua's book in the Bible, it speaks about the sudden destruction of the city of Jericho and the simultaneous great escape of Rachel and her family (and whomever else she invited to wait for escape in her house on the wall). It is a miracle that only one section of the wall was spared. It was not a chance factor, however, that only the portion of the city's wall where her house was located did not fall down flat. Having been promised in the Biblical narrative that she would escape if she did what she was told by the two Jewish spies, she believed, she did, and she escaped.

It is noteworthy that when the walls of the city fell down, the Bible says they fell down flat. The wall did not fall over in littered stacked up piles of brick as one would think. Recent excavations show that somehow the walls were pushed down into the ground, presumably so that the Israelite army encircling the city could go up quickly into the city and decimate it. Here again we have an illustration that the Israelite warriors who were protected by God went up into the city and rescued Rahab from death on the same day of destruction of the earth-dwellers in Jericho [Joshua 6:17].

Example #4 – Moses and Israel

We find in the story of the Exodus that the fleeing children of Israel who were escaping from Egypt is another example of sudden destruction and escape occurring on the same day. In Exodus 14:27-31 we read that Moses stretched forth his hand to part the Red Sea for the Israelites to escape through its waters; and he did so again on the other side causing the waters to close upon the huge Egyptian army whereby every single one of them including Pharaoh drowned [Exodus 15:19]. Was it not a 'Day of Destiny' for both the Israelis and the Egyptians?

I submit that through these four examples, God is showing us through Old Testament typology what will happen when He closes the Age of Grace. Recall that the rapture terminates the 'times of the gentiles' known as the Age of Grace; so that God can finish the Age of Israel whose final week of years has been on hold. Paul was aware of these examples which are perhaps the reason he intimated through prophecy in his letter to Thessaly that sudden destruction and rapture would happen on the same day. So, what does that mean for us?

Summary

If we can determine that a sudden destruction is about to occur on planet earth, we can be somewhat confident that our escape from it in rapture will happen as well. Have you been watching the build-up of armies in the Middle East? WWIII is looming on the horizon. Russia is bent on resuming supremacy in her hemisphere. Will the present Middle East conflagration going on now be the sudden destruction of First Thessalonians?

As per Ezekiel 38 and 39, God has put a hook in Russia's jaw and is pulling her down into the Middle East turmoil. In sync with Ezekiel's narrative, Russia is working with Iran and Turkey and appears to be the Gog/Magog warlord of Ezekiel's prophecy. Endtime prophecies are rapidly being fulfilled.

Amazingly, the Covid-19 worldwide pandemic has been touted in the news as a dress rehearsal of how the globalists will execute their one world order. The soft marshal law every nation has experienced has been a trailer (preview) of the Tribulational plagues to come which will pale when the Horseman of Revelation 6:8 rides. Are you prepared for rapture?

Even though we cannot know which day and hour our departure will happen, note the following which indicates we are in the season of the endtimes. Tumultuous violence and anarchy are cropping up everywhere; physical catastrophes from earthquakes, volcanism, and extreme weather events are escalating; massive refugee populations are fleeing persecution; genocide in novel ways is happening in certain parts of the world; economic woes plague every country in the world; and, as has been noted, pandemic outbreaks is being publicized as a new normal.

These are all signs that the labor of earth's pregnancy is at work. They will bring forth a New World Order be it the order of the Antichrist or the Kingdom Age of Jesus. Hence, we should be alert and watchful moreso than ever. Stay close to the Lord through repentance and upright living, for it is the uprightness of a person that delivers and protects from trouble and from missing rapture [Psalms 32:7; 37:17-19].

Is this the time? Jews are expecting a Messiah, but not Jesus Christ. If a so-called Messiah shows up on Israel's doorstep, it will be the Anti-Messiah or Anti-Christ. The Bible prophesies that when Israel accepts a false Messiah as her protector from neighboring pillage, she has engaged the time of Jacob's troubles [Jeremiah 30:7] that will birth the Kingdom Age. But unfortunately, the birth pangs she experiences will be the worst holocaust for the Jewish people ever, in fact, for all earth-dwellers according to Jesus [Matthew 24:21].

Nevertheless, God is gracious and delights in mercy. He loves to forgive repentant people [Psalms 86:5]. Repentance brings Jubilee benefits to obedient children and qualifies one for rapture. But the Father is also a God of truth, justice, and judgment. This part of His essence will bring cursing instead of blessing to whoever refuses to turn away from wickedness aka perversity or wrong thinking to Him.

Make sure you are on the side of freedom and blessing by studying prophecy as in this book so that you stay righteous and holy for your rapture/wedding day. I exhort everyone always to be repentant, to pray, to walk on the highway of holiness that others may see your good works, and to loudly praise God for His merciful-kindnesses which are great toward us all [Psalm 117].

Are You Rapture-Ready?

CHAPTER -8

WHO IS QUALIFIED FOR RAPTURE?

The Case has been made that a Pretribulational rapture answers best the many prophetic Scriptures concerning Jesus' Second Advent to earth to rebuild the house of David that is fallen down [Acts 15:16], which house peaked under King Solomon's rule. An important discovery from studying the whole counsel of God is that Jesus' return to rebuild David's house and to establish Israel's Kingdom Age of a thousand-years rule occurs in two phases.

If Jesus doesn't come back twice with several years in between, there are at least a dozen Scriptures related to His return that will not harmonize. We have seen in the foregoing chapters the Bible indeed infers that at the beginning of the Tribulation Jesus comes back to just above the mountains to snatch His Bride out of harm's way; and He returns a second time at the end of the seven-years Tribulation when He touches His feet upon the earth.

Because God is perfect, accurate, and absolute truth, everything in His canon of Scripture must harmonize and be fulfilled. Jesus coming back twice easily fulfills the Word of God. Apostle Matthew wrote in his gospel that with His First Advent Jesus fulfilled Scripture 16 times (in my King James Version). And there are 41 other verses confirming *'that it might be fulfilled'* in other books of the New Testament concerning His First Appearance.

Whatever interpretations of prophetic Scripture are proferred must bring into agreement all prophecy. They must allow for fulfillment all passages of Scripture without inconveniencing others as they did for His First Advent.

For example, scribes in Jesus' day thought Nazareth was His birth place and that Joseph was His father; but when the veil was rent and truth revealed, people discovered those were inaccurate notions. The closer one gets to a destination, the clearer the signs become. Since we are in the season of rapture, the Pretribulational position for rapture is accommodating better in my estimation the prophetic Scriptures about our Lord's return.

We must not disdain others for seeing things differently than we do, however. The facts are not all in yet. Any one of us could be wrong. Nonetheless, our Lord forewarns us to be alert, watchful, and continue instant looking for a translation out of this present world into the spirit realm which means we must search the Scriptures for evidence of when rapture might happen. That is a major reason this book exists.

Jesus chastised the scribes and Pharisees for not recognizing that He, the Messiah, was standing right before their eyes. The myriad of miraculous works were evidence of who He was [John 5:36, 39-40]. Let us not repeat their mistake now that the signs show His return upon us.

From the foregoing chapters, it is plain that not all Christians are going to be raptured. Given that rapture is code for the marriage of the Lamb of God, and given that Christians who qualify for rapture are the Lamb's Bride, let's find out who is eligible to be in the Bridehood of Jesus.

Eternal Life Is Required To Enter Heaven

The very first thing a person must understand is that not everyone who calls himself or herself a Christian is truly a Christian. Many Christians are nominal Christians, i.e., Christian in name only. As will be shown below, the Bible teaches that a person must be born again to become a Christian and enter the Kingdom of Heaven. Sitting in a garage does not make one a car, and sitting in a church building does not make one a Christian. Neither does joining a group in a denomination, building, or house church make one a Christian.

Jesus told the learned Nicodemus, a notable scholar in Jewish circles, point blank that he must be born again to enter the Kingdom of God. He was revealing to Nicodemus a spiritual truth so that it could be recorded in Scripture as it is here to inform people down through time how to obtain Eternal life, the purpose for which Nicodemus sought Jesus' wisdom [John 3:3 with 3:7].

In fact, seeking salvation in Old Testament times embodied a search by persons of all religious faiths for the Holy Grail of Everlasting Life. For proof that people were concerned about it read: John 3:14-16; 5:39; 6:68; 10:38; 17:2; Mark 10:17; Acts 10:48; Romans 6:23; Titus 1:2; 1 John 2:25; 5:20]. Other Scriptures could be cited but those are enough to prove that the quest of most people ever since Adam sinned and brought death has been to find a way to overcome death and obtain Eternal Life.

John 3:5-8
5 Jesus answered (*Nicodemus*), Verily, verily, I say unto thee, Except a man be born of water (*the flesh*) and

(*also*) of the Spirit, he cannot enter into the kingdom of God.

6 That which is born of the flesh is flesh; and that which is born of the Spirit is spirit.

7 Marvel not that I said unto thee, Ye must be born again.

8 The wind bloweth where it listeth, and thou hearest the sound thereof, but canst not tell whence it cometh, and whither it goeth: so is every one that is born of the Spirit.

The spirit realm is invisible although somewhat perceptive to the physical senses as verse 8 teaches. This means that whatever happens in the spirit realm such as a spiritual birth must be revealed to man through revelation knowledge. Jesus was giving Nicodemus revelation knowledge when He told him that the requirement for entering heaven was becoming spiritually reborn at which time a person's new spirit possesses Eternal Life. Hence, Eternal Life and being spiritually reborn are the same thing.

Jesus explained to Nicodemus that in the life of a human being two births are necessary to live eternally. The Master said that the first birth is a natural physical birth called being born of the flesh, and the second birth is called a spiritual birth [verse 6].

Babies and young children are spiritually alive to God because they have not sinned. So when they die, they automatically go to heaven. Being in the preoperational stage of human development young children cannot compute two variables at the same time. But when they move into the operational stage of intellectual development (developmental stages vary in age with the sophistication of a culture), they can compute two variables at once – variable #1) awareness that a commandment is made, and variable #2) disobedience to it will bring punishment.

When conflation of variables occur – a commandment is given and the child deliberately disobeys knowing disobedience will bring punishment – sin revives and the person dies. God alone knows when this happens with each person.

Romans 7:9
9 For I was alive without the law once: but when the commandment came, sin revived, and I died.

Apostle Paul explains in his Roman letter the reason that people must be born again. To summarize his discourse tersely, it is the spirit in a person that needs to be revived to life, i.e., born again. Paul shows in his Roman thesis that Jesus came to rectify the dilemma of man. People are dead because of sin and cannot extract themselves out of it [Romans 3:23 with 6:23]. But God sent His Son Jesus to redeem humanity from its predicament. Very simply, God offers Jesus' death as a substitute for the sin debt man owes God. It is a gift freely given from God's heart of love for His creation.

It is obvious that even though the spirit dies, the body is still alive in like manner that Adam and Eve were still physically alive after disobeying God. They died spiritually immediately. But their bodies lived on for several hundreds of years before they died physically. We do not have such luxury of existence today. At most a man might live to be as old as Moses who died at 120 years of age. But in reality, every person is only one breath away from eternity.

Given the above, the first qualification for making rapture is to be spiritually reborn. According to Jesus in the foregoing chat about Eternal Life, a person cannot enter the Kingdom of

God without it. Therefore, Jesus comes for people already converted to Christianity through belief in Him as the Savior of lost men [Romans 10:13].

1 John 5:11-12

11 And this is the record, that God hath given to us eternal life, and this life is in his Son.

12 He that hath the Son hath life; and he that hath not the Son of God hath not life.

Considering that apostle Paul's Roman road agrees with apostle John's quote above, a person needs to make sure he possesses Eternal Life now in the devil's cosmic system. It behooves one to find out about his or her spiritual status because whatever state one is in at death is the destiny of one's spirit. Born-again people go to heaven, the place of love-natured spirits; and people without a rebirth will go to the home of their sin-natured lord aka satan. Therefore, one must decide before death where He wants to spend eternity.

Spiritual welfare involves spending time with the Lord in private to discern truths by meditating Scripture from the Christian Bible as opposed to seeking worldly facts which change with every new scientific discovery. Truth never changes. God's Word is truth and is forever settled in heaven [Psalms 119:89].

It would help a seeker of Eternal Life to time stamp his having acted upon God's gracious offer of salvation through Jesus Christ. See the Addendum for better clarity regarding how to become a Christian and settle the issue once and for all.

133

The next step after obtaining Eternal Life is renewing the mind. Before salvation, everything a person learned is tied to an old sin-natured spirit. At salvation a believer's sin-natured spirit dies with Jesus on the cross of Calvary [Ephesians 2:5, 6]. When a believer receives Jesus as His Savior, his spirit is reconfigured into a love nature like His new Father's from above which is the reason old behaviors need changing.

The essence of a spirit renewal amounts to having the frequencies of a person's DNA transformed to match that of his new heavenly Father's. This is a triumphant tour de force only God can accomplish. Nonetheless, habits and attitudes acquired before the new birth remain intact in the intellect and continue to direct one's behavior until their schemata implanted in the brain's cortical structures are changed.

Old habits and motivations embedded in the brain must be replaced or one is doomed to die spiritually retarded and bereft of rewards in the afterlife. Exchange of cortical structures is done by acting or doing things [James 1:22] based on God's methods as taught by the Scriptures [Isaiah 55:8, 9]. Learning through Bible study the difference between the ways of God and the ways of the world is critical for living life free from bondages to sin, sickness, disease, and lack. This new divine life flow prepares one for rapture.

Wherefore, the first step to renewed thinking is understanding that humans are tripartite beings. According to 1 Thessalonians 5:23, humans are spirits who live in bodies and have souls which mediate between the body and the spirit. Because God created man in the likeness of Himself, man is a spirit [John 4:24]. God wanted people to be in His likeness so

He could fellowship with them as they took dominion of the earth in a Father-Son business-like operation.

Genesis 1:26
26 And God said, Let us make <u>man in our image, after our likeness</u>: and let them <u>have dominion</u> over the fish of the sea, and over the fowl of the air, and over the cattle, and over all the earth, and over every creeping thing that creepeth upon the earth.

In the above statement, God teaches that man was created in His class and was given dominion over His works. Creating humans in God's class is what caused Lucifer aka satan to sin. He was jealous that a creature with less strength, size, acumen, and musical aptitude than he had could share God's power on an equal basis with God. Angels were not created in God's class. So, pride coupled with jealousy was the bane of satan's fall. Read Isaiah 14:12-17 and Ezekiel 28:11-19 to learn about it.

This book about rapture does not require one to understand the history of man's fall. What is required is that you know not all Christians will be raptured since many people who call themselves Christian have never been born again; and other people claiming Christianity are unprepared for rapture. When talking with people about salvation, I never ask if they are a Christian; I ask if they have been born again.

I have read testimonies of pastors who admit that after retiring from years of service they found out they were Christian in name only. I wonder how many went to their graves without having been reborn into the Christian faith?

The purpose of this final chapter is to let the reader know that to be in the Bridehood of Jesus, one must be in the family of God through a spiritual rebirth since Jesus, the Christ, is coming for a Christian Bride. This involves making a deliberate choice to serve God and not the world.

Once in the family, the next step is to renew the mind through meditating and studying Scripture. Without renewal, it is impossible to know how to please God by not sinning and how to remain distant from worldliness which is enmity with God [James 4:4]. Hence, becoming rapture-ready requires continual repentance from dead works.

Paul affirms the above exhortation because he said to ...

Romans 12:2
2 ...be not conformed to this world: but be ye transformed by the renewing of your mind...

Transformation involves repentance, a changing of one's thoughts about something. It is the means of becoming born again. The Holy Spirit convicts people of the one sin that condemns a person to eternal separation from God – the sin of not believing that Jesus paid the sin debt owed God.

Read it for yourself: *And when he* (the Holy Spirit) *is come, he will reprove the world of sin,...of sin because they believe not on me* [John 16:8, 9]. The word 'sin' in both verses 8 and 9 is singular in the original Greek text indicating that the reference is to only one sin, the sin of rejecting God's method of salvation.

After that, repentance is a perpetual changing of the mind regarding how one lives life in the devil's cosmic system. Meditation in the Word will reveal what needs changing. Choosing daily to follow God's ways of doing things instead of the world's will keep one rapture-ready.

The degree to which one buys into the world's way of doing things is the measure of hindrance leading away from God and rapture. Let me repeat so you don't miss it, discernment about how God's methods differ from the world's methods [Isaiah 55:8, 9] can only be obtained through study and meditation in the Word of God.

Space does not permit delving any deeper into this necessity of making proper choices for divine living and rapture-readiness. Perhaps another book is needed that can aid a believer in making certain his choices do not impede membership in the Bridehood of Christ. It is sufficient to say at this time that God is merciful and gracious and looks on the heart. So, if you are wanting to do right although stumbling, it is accounted to you for righteousness.

In Closing…

Everyone that's born into the world is given a megabucks winning lottery ticket into heaven, for …*God is not willing that any perish but that all should come to repentance* [2 Peter 3:9]. All one has to do to cash his ticket and live abundantly [John 10:10] is to acknowledge that Jesus is the Lord of one's life.

After a decision to receive the gifted ticket with its incredible riches, the next choice a believer must make aligns with the quest of this book which is to determine whether it is cashable at rapture or at resurrection. It's a sure-fire win because Jesus has paid the price for all the riches included in the ticket, riches for the here and now as well as in the afterlife, riches for whatever we need and for whatever we want that does not violate 'the Will' of God.

According to Apostle Peter, all believers have been blessed with …*all things pertaining to life and godliness* [1 Peter 2:3, 4] which are the 'whatevers' of the foregoing that has been furnished through the work of Jesus on the cross. That's grace folks and shouting ground. There is nothing we can add to what God has already provided for us. Praising God continually for the riches of His grace will go a long way in keeping one ready for rapture.

Be cautious, however, not to flaunt God's grace riches with a hyper-grace superior attitude, for the Lord gives more and more grace to the humble but resists the proud [James 4:6; 1 Peter 5:5]. So, rapturite hopefuls be careful to stay humble. Thinking pridefully because of one's righteous standing with God might disqualify a person for rapture since God resists the proud.

The way to kill pride and arrogancy because of one's new standing as a son or daughter of God Almighty with unlimited ability is to walk in love. If you love God, love your neighbor, and do unto others as you want them to do unto you, you have fulfilled the whole law and the only commandment of the New Covenant – to love one another as Jesus loved [John 13:34].

Watch how Jesus lived life because He perfectly illustrated the love walk. He handled His knowledge of who he was, God's Son, perfectly by being totally committed to doing His Father's will. He modeled the way God wants all His children to act. He knew He was the Messiah and possessed heavenly throne-room power, yet He always humbly gave God the glory for whatever miraculous wonders He performed. Although He could have, He never exalted Himself.

Typically when a person knows someone highly influential is coming to see them, they scurry around checking to see that everything is in place. orderly, and clean. This ought to be the attitude of every rapturite in this season of the Lord's return to establish His Kingdom. Time is of essence now because the confluence of signs and signals indicates that Jesus is on the threshold of heaven's open door.

Hopefully, the reader has learned that whoever wants to be raptured can be. It's a matter of making proper choices. God has not excluded anyone the opportunity to partake of Eternal Life and hence rapture. He loves all His creatures and has made it known in His self-revelation called the Bible.

I hope to meet you in heaven….or, on the way up in rapture.

EPILOGUE

Since there are so many converging earthly signs and heavenly signals pointing to Jesus' Second Advent to earth, we should be living out of a hustle mentality of getting ourselves prepared for rapture. Like as in sports' games, teams speed up their efforts to win just before the end. A clock is a coach's most prized possession in the last stretch of a competition.

Given all the Scriptural evidence in the preceding chapters of this book, everyone who has the hope of seeing the Lord in rapture *purifies himself even as he is pure*.

1 John 3:2-3
2 Beloved, now are we the sons of God, and it doth not yet appear what we shall be: but we know that, when he shall appear (*to rapture His Bride*), we shall be like him; for we shall see him as he is.
3 And every man that hath this hope in him purifieth himself, even as he is pure.

Whose appearance should rapturites be mimicking? They ought to be as godly, holy, and righteous as Jesus who is coming to snatch His Bride off earth before Tribulation begins. It can't be talking about the end of the Tribulation era because by that time there will not be many people left on earth who survive the onslaughts of terror seizing the populace. Focus will be primarily on survival, not cleansing from worldliness.

The Greek word for 'purifieth' is *hagnos* and means to be unspoiled or untarnished by the world's way of doing things. By the end of Tribulation there will be very little left to lust after in the world. Hence, self-purification to meet the Lord in the above passage of Scripture is bespeaking of rapture. It is now in our current society that worldly things entice people to sin and consort with its ways.

Awareness about imminent rapture brings joy to saints who contemplate seeing the Lord face-to-face. Because a Christian's strength is tied to his/her joy [Nehemiah 8:10], God provides signs so he or she can make adjustments in preparation for meeting Jesus. Like road signs, the closer to a destination, the more road signs there are. Christians who aren't wholeheartedly looking for Him might misread the signs and perhaps miss rapture.

How does one prepare for rapture? Get rid of all sin that you are aware of, and stay away from worldliness which can stain a cleansed persona. Spend more time fellowshipping with the Lord; for it is through a close relationship acquired through frequent communing that one is able to hear the Lord whisper in His still small voice [1 Kings 19:12] when things are about to happen [John 16:13].

The degree of attention one gives to the things of the world and of the flesh is the measure of hindrance preventing a person from experiencing what is real and from hearing the Spirit guide what to do and what to avoid. Buying into the world's way of doing things automatically keeps one from being sensitive to the things of the spirit realm where our eternal home is located.

In other words, flowing with the world is walking in shadows that have no enduring substance. The day is coming when the entire physical realm will disappear because it is temporal without eternal materiality [2 Peter 3:10-12]. That's the reason the Bible teaches worldly mindedness is enmity with God and leads to death [Romans 8:7; James 4:4].

The conclusion of this book, therefore, is to reverence God, keep his commandments, and stay rapture-ready. And remember that rapture is not an ending, it's a beginning. It's the start of our Everlasting Life with our Father-God, the source of Eternal Life.

HOW TO BECOME A CHRISTIAN

If you have gone to the altar time and again in order to get saved expecting that you would feel something, yet felt nothing, you are operating on the wrong wavelength. You are looking to feelings, that is, emotions instead of reasoning to save you. Salvation is never dependent upon how one feels, but upon what one believes. Salvation is a gift, and it does not depend upon you. Everything depends upon God and what He has said in His *unchangeable* Word about how to be saved and obtain Eternal Life: *In hope of <u>Eternal Life,</u> which <u>God, that cannot lie, promised </u>before the world began* [Titus 1:2]. Note the following instructions...

Romans 10:9-10
9 That if thou shalt confess with thy mouth the Lord Jesus, and shalt believe in thine heart that God hath raised him from the dead, thou shalt be saved.
10 For with the heart man believeth unto righteousness; and <u>with the mouth confession is made unto salvation</u>.

One believes in the <u>mind</u>. Never does the Bible anywhere say you must <u>feel</u> something to be saved. You may or may not feel anything. The key is to believe. Feelings follow faith.

John 3:36

36 He that believeth on the Son hath everlasting life: and he that believeth not the Son shall not see life; but the wrath of God **abideth** on him.

The Bible teaches we must be regenerated, i.e., born again. This means the Holy Spirit reconfigures our sin nature to match the love nature of Jesus; thus, our minds need renewing [Ephesians 4:23]. Both regeneration and renewing imply a change. In effect, it is the result of having changed masters, of having changed one's mind about whom to serve – God or the devil.

Jesus taught that there are only two masters; therefore, only the deluded think they are the masters of their own destiny. If you have not believed on the Son of God and made Him Lord of your life, you are **abiding** with the wrath of God already on you according to the above. The Greek word for 'abide' is a present tense verb meaning that you stand condemned already in this present reality necessitating a decision to change Lordships. One must be translated out of Satan's kingdom of darkness and transferred into the kingdom of Jesus [Colossians 1:13].

As noted above, God created feelings to respond or react to what one thinks. A person has to know he is insulted to get angry; he has to know there was a goof-up to feel foolish; he has to understand he is blessed to feel joy; and he has to understand he is a sinner to feel remorse. Feeling remorseful does not save you, however. Judas felt remorse and hanged himself. Can you see that emotions or feelings are responders and not initiators?

Feeling helpless and lost must be accompanied by the will to change, and this is what the Bible calls repentance. It is what you believe or think that counts. People need to **know** they are sinners and need saving.

Isaiah 53:6
6 All we like sheep have gone astray; we have turned every one to his own way; and the LORD hath laid on him (*Jesus*) the iniquity of us all.

The wages of sin is death [Romans 6:23], and again, *for all have sinned and come short of the glory of God* [Romans 3:23] are Scriptures that teach the helpless condition of man. The devils believe Jesus is God's Son [Luke 4:41] and tremble [James 2:19]. So there must be something more to salvation than just mental assent. It involves a total commitment to Jesus and to unashamedly confess Him as Lord [Matthew 10:32, 33].

You may have been told that you must **do** something or give up some things in order to be saved. That is not what the Bible teaches. After salvation, you probably will want to get rid of some shackles and ungodly habits, but that is after the fact. It is not what you do that saves you but what you receive. Salvation is a gift freely given to all who want it.

Ephesians 2:8-9
8 For by grace are ye saved through faith; and that not of yourselves: it is the gift of God:

9 Not of works, lest any man should boast.

Again in John 1:12: *But as many as **received** Him, to them gave he power to become the Sons of God, even to them that believe on His name*. From these scriptures (and there are many more like them) you can see that salvation is <u>a **gift** to be received</u>. If one must do anything to accept the gift, the concept of 'gift' is nullified. God said, C*ome now, and let us **reason** together.* Notice that it does <u>not</u> say emote together. *Though your sins be as scarlet, they shall be as white as snow, though they be red like crimson, they shall be as wool* [Isaiah 1:18]. We need to use our **reasoning** faculties and not our emotions to get saved.

It takes no effort to have faith. A little child has faith, and that is why Jesus said unless we become as little children we cannot enter the Kingdom of God. *Verily I say unto you, except ye be converted, and become as little children, ye shall not enter into the kingdom of heaven* [Matthew 18:3]. The Father has made salvation so simple it takes help to misunderstand it. Oftentimes highly educated people stumble at salvation, for they are prone to want to add to what Jesus has done on the cross. Jesus alone paid the penalty for the sins of the world [Hebrews 1:3]; and he alone reconciled humanity to God the Father. We cannot even leave a tip.

*All things are **of God**, who has reconciled us **to Himself** by Jesus Christ.* Amazingly, God is not imputing any trespasses unto us [2 Corinthians 5:18, 19]. Through Jesus' work of the cross, separation from God due to sin ended; thus, we qualify to receive the righteousness of God. *For he* (God) *hath made* *him* (Jesus) *to be sin for us, who knew no sin; that we might be made the righteousness of God in him* [5:21]. Since the Father Himself declared justice has been met through Jesus' suffering on the cross [Isaiah 53:11], who can deny it?

Because sin is no longer an issue, and because the work of making peace with God is accomplished, every person alive has the opportunity, yes even responsibility, to receive salvation and to become a member of the family of God and citizen of the Kingdom of Heaven.

Are you wondering if there is anything that must be done besides believing to be saved? There is one thing. You must confess with your mouth that you want to become a child of God. If you have trouble knowing how to put it in words, read the simple prayer at the end of these instructions, which if spoken **sincerely and truthfully** will get you born again. (Also, read Chapter 3 of the Gospel of John to understand the necessity of being born again.)

Heed this word of warning. Proverbs 29:1 says: *He, that being often reproved who hardeneth his neck, shall suddenly be destroyed, and that without remedy.* God **now** stands ready to pity you. In this day of mercy you have hope. But, there is coming a day when the unsaved will be totally lost, abandoned by God, reprobate and without hope of neither heaven nor Eternal Life. The Bible teaches that death and misery are the final states of the unregenerate.

Read Proverbs 1:24-33 for a vivid account of God's anger when one spurns His offer of free salvation, of refusing grace now. He will not pity or have mercy on them because having called them to repentance, refusal of His grace will condemn them. Jesus said not once but twice, in Luke 13:3 and 5, that *...except ye repent, ye shall <u>all</u> likewise perish.* All means everyone. The Bible tells us repeatedly that God is no respecter of persons. If the matchless love of the Son of God who laid down His divine life on a cross so that you and I could be saved does not move you to repentance, then, perhaps the dreadful thought of an <u>endless life</u> separated from all vestige of love, goodness, grace and glory will.

Dear reader, awaken to the danger of a careless life walking a tightrope between heaven and hell. Consider the Lord's stern warnings about coming judgment:

John 5:24-30
24 Verily, verily, I say unto you, He that heareth my word, and believeth on him that sent me, hath everlasting life, and shall not come into condemnation; but is passed from death unto life.
25 Verily, verily, I say unto you, The hour is coming, and now is, when the dead shall hear the voice of the Son of God: and they that hear shall live.
26 For as the Father hath life in himself; so hath he given to the Son to have life in himself;
27 And hath given him authority to execute judgment also, because he is the Son of man.
28 Marvel not at this: for the hour is coming, in the which all that are in the graves shall hear his voice,

29 And shall come forth; they that have done good, unto the resurrection of life; and they that have done evil, unto the resurrection of damnation.

30 I can of mine own self do nothing: as I hear, I judge: and my judgment is just; because I seek not mine own will, but the will of the Father which hath sent me.

Do not put off calling upon Jesus to save you because according to verse 30 above Jesus cannot help you. He cannot believe for you. In Matthew 12:37 He said, *by thy words thou shalt be justified, and by thy words thou shalt be condemned.* Jesus has done everything He can do. He gave His all. He gave His life. But be aware that repentance costs. Changing kingdoms from the kingdom of darkness to the kingdom of light and life requires different protocols and standards. The glories of the kingdom of light are worth it. Remember that each of us is only one breath away from eternity. Life literally hangs by a thread. It can snap at any moment. God invites you to repeat the prayer that follows and enjoy the riches of heaven.

Dear Heavenly Father,

I call upon you to save me. You said, him *that cometh to me I will in no wise cast out* [John 6:37], and *whosoever shall call upon the name of the Lord* (Jesus) *shall be saved* [Romans 10:13]. I believe that you will not refuse me entrance into your Kingdom. I am taking you at your Word because I know you cannot lie [Titus 1:2].

I believe in my heart that Jesus Christ is your Son, and I believe that He died on the cross for my sins. I also believe that He was raised from the dead for my justification so that I might have Eternal Life. I am now calling upon you Jesus to save me from the requirement that I pay for my own sins. I understand that I am a sinner and need to be saved. I accept your Word that says salvation is a freely offered gift received by faith. I receive it now in the privacy of my own convictions.

I accept your Word that salvation is not a question of how I feel, but a question of what I believe. Thank you Father for making it so simple. Thank you Jesus for loving me so deeply you died in my place. I confess you Jesus as my Lord. I renounce all attachment to Satan, and I fully believe that I am now a child of the living God.

I ask you to help me learn to walk uprightly as a new person and to make right choices. I do not want to sin any longer, and I want to be ready to meet you Jesus in the rapture. I want to be where you are in heavenly Jerusalem. Please cleanse me and give me a desire for the things that are eternal. I know you will because you are now my Father, and a good Father always wants the best for his children. Thank you for making it possible for my name to be written in heaven not only as a citizen of your Kingdom but also and more importantly for making it possible for me to become an adopted child in your family, a joint heir with Jesus of all things. Praise God, I am saved.

I pray this prayer in Jesus' name. Amen.

Signed: ______________________________________

Dated : ______________________________________

If you have prayed the prayer above, I suggest you acknowledge it (we must confess Jesus before someone) by telling your pastor, a friend, your family, or the next stranger you meet.

Luke 12:8-9

8 Also I say unto you, Whosoever shall confess me before men, him shall the Son of man also confess before the angels of God:

9 But he that denieth me before men shall be denied before the angels of God.

Now that you are saved, the next step is to renew your mind to the Word of God [Romans 12:2] so that you can learn about how spiritually powerful you are because your identity is now in Jesus. Further, the Bible will teach you how to access Kingdom benefits in this present world before entering heaven since they are part of your eternal inheritance. May the Lord greatly bless you in your new walk with Jesus.